Date of Return	Date of Return	Date of Return

ADAM AND EVE AND PINCH ME

by A. E. Coppard

(595)

ADAM AND EVE
AND PINCH ME

Tales by
A. E. COPPARD

PENGUIN BOOKS

HARMONDSWORTH MIDDLESEX ENGLAND
254 FIFTH AVENUE NEW YORK U.S.A.

First published 1921
Published in Penguin Books 1946

MADE AND PRINTED IN GREAT BRITAIN FOR PENGUIN BOOKS LTD.,
BY HUNT, BARNARD AND CO., LTD., LONDON AND AYLESBURY

to

LILY ANNE

OTHER BOOKS BY A. E. COPPARD

✻ ✻ ✻

CONTENTS

MARCHING TO ZION

In the great days that are gone I was walking the Journey upon its easy smiling roads and came one morning of windy spring to the side of a wood. I had but just rested to eat my crusts and suck a drink from the pool when a fat woman appeared and sat down before me. I gave her the grace of the morning.

'And how many miles is it now?' I asked of her.

'What!' said she, 'you're not going the journey?'

'Sure, ma'am,' said I, 'I'm going, and you're going, and we're all going . . . aren't we?'

'Not,' said she, looking at me very archly, 'not while there are well-looking young fellers sitting in the woods.'

'Well, deliver me!' said I, 'd'ye take me for the Angel Gabriel or the duke of the world!'

'It's not anything I'm taking you to be, young man . . . give me a chew of that bread.'

She came and sat beside me and took it from my hands.

'Little woman . . .' I began it to her; but at

that she flung the crust back in my face, laughing
and choking and screaming.

'Me . . . that's fat as a ewe in January!'

'Fat, woman!' says I, 'you're not fat at all.'

But, I declare it, she'd a bosom like a bolster.
I lay on my back beside her. She was a rag of a
woman. I looked up through the tree branches at
the end of the shaw; they were bare, spring was
late that year. The sky was that blue . . . there
wasn't a cloud within a million miles . . . but up
through the boughs it looked hard and steely like a
storm sky. I took my hat from her, for she had put
it on her own head, and I stood on my feet.

'Fat, ma'am!' says I . . . and she looked up at
me, grinning like a stuffed fox. . . . 'Oh, no,
ma'am, you're slim as the queen of Egypt!'

At that she called out to another man who was
passing us by, and I went to walk on with him. He
had a furuncle on one side of his chin; his garments
were very old, both in fashion and in use; he was
lean as a mountain cow.

I greeted him, but he gave me glances that were
surly, like a man would be grinding scissors or
setting a saw—for you never met one of that kind
that didn't have the woe of the world upon him.

'How many miles is it now, sir?' I asked, very

respectful then. He did not heed me. He put his
hand to his ear signifying deafness. I shouted and I
shouted, so you could have heard me in the four
kingdoms, but I might just have been blowing in a
sack for all the reason I got from him.

I went on alone and in the course of the days I
fell in with many persons: stupid persons, great
persons, jaunty ones. An ass passes me by, its cart
burdened with a few dead sprays of larch and a log
for the firing. An old man toils at the side urging
the ass onwards. They give me no direction and I
wonder whether I am at all like the ass, or the man,
or the cart, or the log for the firing. I cannot say.
There was the lad McGlosky, who had the fine
hound that would even catch birds; the philosopher
who had two minds; the widow with one leg;
Slatterby Chough, the pugfoot man, and Grafton.
I passed a little time with them all, and made poems
about them that they did not like, but I was ever
for walking on from them. None of them could
give me a direction for the thing that was urging me
except that it was 'away on, away on'.

Walk I did, and it was full summer when I met
Monk, the fat fellow as big as two men with but
the clothes of a small one squeezing the joints of him
together. Would you look at the hair of him—it

was light as a stook of rye; or the face of him and the neck of him—the hue of a new brick. He had the mind of a grasshopper, the strength of a dray-horse, the tenderness of a bush of reeds, and was light on his limbs as a deer.

'Look ye're,' he said to me; he had a stiff sort of talk, and fat thumbs like a mason that he jiggled in the corners of his pockets; 'look ye're, my friend, my name is Monk.'

'I am Michael Fionnguisa,' said I.

'Well I never struck fist with a lad like you; your conversation is agreeable to me, you have a stride on you would beat the world for greatness.'

'I could beat you,' said I, 'even if you wore the boots of Hermes that had wings on 'em.'

'It is what I like,' said he, and he made a great mess of my boasting before we were through. 'Look ye're, my friend, we needn't brag our little eye-blink of the world; but take my general char-acter and you'll find I'm better than my . . . inferiors. I accomplish my ridiculous destiny with-out any ridiculous effort. I'm the man to go a-travelling with.'

He had that stiff way of his talk, like a man lectur-ing on a stool; but my mercy, he'd a tongue of silk that could twist a meal out of the pantry of Jews and strange hard people; fat landladies, the wives of the street, the widows in their villas, they would feed him until he groaned, loving him for his blitheness and his tales. He could not know the meaning of want though he had never a coin in the world. Yet he did not love towns; he would walk wide-eyed through them counting the seams in the pavements. He liked most to be staring at the gallant fishes in the streams, and gasping when he saw a great one.

I met him in the hills and we were gone together. And it was not a great while before he was doing and doing, for we came and saw a man committing a crime—a grave crime to be done in a bad world leave alone a good one like this—in a very lonely, lovely place. So Monk rose up and slew him, and the woman ran blushing into the woods.

I looked at Mr. Monk, and the dead man on the road, and then at Mr. Monk again.

'Well,' I said, 'we'd . . . we'd better bury this feller.'

But Monk went and sat upon a bank and wiped his neck. The other lay upon his face as if he were sniffing at the road; I could see his ear was full of blood, it slipped over the lobe drip by drip as neat as a clock would tick.

And Monk, he said: 'Look ye're, my friend, there are dirtier things than dirt, and I would not like to mix this with the earth of our country.'

So we slung him into an old well with a stone upon his loins.

And a time after that we saw another man committing crime, a mean crime that you might do and welcome in America or some such region, but was not fitting to be done in our country.

So Monk rose up and slew him. Awful it was to see what Monk did to him. He was a great killer and fighter; Hector himself was but a bit of a page-boy to Mr. Monk.

'Shall we give him an interment?' I asked him. He stood wiping his neck—he was always wiping his neck—and Monk, he said:

'Look ye're, my friend, he was a beast; a man needn't live in a sty in order to become a pig, and we won't give him an interment.' So we heaved him into a slag-pit, among rats and ravels of iron.

And would you believe it, again we saw a man committing crime, crime indeed and a very bad crime.

There was no withstanding Monk; he rose up and slew the man as dead as the poor beast he had tortured.

[6]

'God-a-mercy!' I said to him, 'it's a lot of life you're taking, Mr. Monk.'

And Monk, he said: 'Life, Michael dear, is the thing we perish by.' He had the most terrible angers and yet was kind, kind; nothing could exceed the greatness of his mind or the vigour of his limbs.

Those were the three combats of Monk, but he was changed from that out. Whenever we came to any habitations now he would not call at back doors, nor go stravaiging in yards for odd pieces to eat, but he would go gallantly into an inn and offer his payment for the things we would like. I could not understand it at all, but he was a great man and a kind.

'Where did you get that treasure?' said I to him after days of it. 'Has some noble person given you a gift?'

He did not answer me, so I asked him over again. 'Eh!'

And Monk, he said: 'Oh well then, there was a lot of coin in the fob of that feller we chucked in the well.'

I looked very straight at Mr. Monk, very straight at that, but I could not speak the things my mind wanted me to say, and he said very artfully: 'Don't distress yourself, Michael dear, over a little contest between sense and sentiment.'

'But that was the dirty man,' said I.

'And why not?' said he. 'If his deed was dirty, his money was clean: don't be deethery, man.'

''Tis not fitting nor honourable,' said I, 'for men the like of us to grow fat on his filth. It's grass I'd be eating sooner.'

'That's all bombazine, Michael, bombazine! I got two dollars more from the feller we chucked in the pit!'

'Mr. Monk, that was the pig!' said I.

'And why not?' said he. 'If his life was bad, then his end must be good: don't be deethery.'

'You can't touch pitch,' I said. . . .

'Who's touching pitch?' he cried. 'Amn't I entitled to the spoils of the valiant, the rewards of the conqueror. . . .'

'Bombazine!' says I to him.

'O begod!' he says, 'I never struck fist on a lad the like of you, with your bombazine O! I grant you it doesn't come affable like, but what costs you nothing can't be dear; as for compunctions, you'll see, I fatten on 'em!'

He laughed outright at me.

[8]

'Don't be deethery, Michael, there was a good
purse in the last man's trousers!'

I could no more complain to him; how could
I under the Lord! Dear me, it never was seen, a
man with the skin of that man; he'd the mind of a
grasshopper, but there was greatness in him, and
Mary herself loved him for a friend.

What do I say about Mary! Ah, there was never
in anything that had the aspects of a world a girl
with her loveliness, I tell you, handsome as a lily,
the jewel of the world; and the thing that happened
between us was strange above all reckoning. We
gave her the good will of the evening in a place that
would be as grand as Eden itself, though the bushes
had grown dim on the hills and the sod was darken-
ing beside the white water of the streams.

'And are you going the Journey?' we asked of
her.

'I am going,' said she, 'everybody is going, why
not me too?'

'Will you go along with us?' I asked of her.

She turned her eyes upon me like two sparks out
of the blowing dusk that was already upon us.

'Yes, I will go with you.'

At that she rested her hand upon my arm and we
turned upon the road together.

[9]

She was barefooted and bareheaded, dressed in a yellow gown that had buttons of ivory upon it.

And we asked her as we went along the streams: Had she no fear of the night-time?

'When the four ends of the world drop on you like death?' says I.

'. . . and the fogs rise up on you like moving grief?' says he.

'. . . and you hear the hoofs of the half-god whisking behind the hedges,' says I.

'. . . and there are bad things like bats troubling the air!' says he.

'. . . or the twig of a tree comes and touches you like a finger!' says I.

'. . . the finger of some meditating doom!' says he.

'No, I am not,' cried Mary, 'but I am glad to be going with you.'

Her hand was again resting upon my arm.

I lay down among the sheaves of wheat that night with no sleep coming to me, for the stars were spilling all out of the sky and it seemed the richness of heaven was flowing down upon us all.

'Michael!' Monk whispered, 'she's a holy-minded girl: look, look, she's praying!'

Sure enough I could see her a little way off, standing like a saint, as still as a monument.

Fresh as a bird was our gentle comrade in the dawn and ready to be going. And we asked her as we went by the roads together: What was it made her to come the Journey alone?

'Sure there is no loneliness in the world,' she said.

'Is there not?' asked Monk.

'I take my soul with me upon this Journey,' said Mary.

'Your what!'

'My soul,' she said gravely, 'it is what keeps loneliness from me.'

He mused upon that a little. 'Look ye're, Mary, soul is just but the chain of eternal mortality, that is what I think it; but you speak as if it were something you pick up and carry about with you, something made of gutta-percha, like a tobacco pouch.'

She smiled upon him: 'It is what covers me from loneliness . . . it's . . . it's the little garment which sometime God will take upon him—being God.'

Seven days only and seven little nights we were together and I made scores of poems about her that were different from any poems that have come into the world, but I could never sing them now. In the mornings she would go wash herself in the pools, and Monk and I would walk a little way off from her. Monk was very delicate about that, but I would turn and see the white-armed girl rolling up her dark hair, and her white feet travelling to the water as she pulled the gown from her beauty. She was made like the down of doves and the bloom of bees. It's like enough she did love me in a very frail and delicate sort of way, like a bush of lavendie might love the wind that would be snaring it from its root in the garden, but never won a petal of it, nor a bloom, only a little of its kind kind air.

We asked her as we went upon the hills: Had she no fear of getting her death?

'Not if I make a wise use of it.'

'A use of your death?—and how would you do that, tell me,' says I.

And she told us grand things about death, in her soft wonderful voice; strange talk to be giving the likes of him and me.

'I'd give the heart out of my skin,' said I, 'not to be growing old—the sin and sorrow of the world, with no hope in life and despair in its conclusion.'

But Monk was full of laughter at me.

'Ha! ha! better a last hope than a hopeless conclusion,' says Mr. Monk; 'so try hope with another lozenge, Michael, and give a free drink to despair.'

[12]

'Have *you* no fear of death?' Mary asked of him.

And Monk, he said: 'I have no unreasonable regard for him; I may bow before the inevitable, but I decline to grovel before it, and if I burn with the best of 'em—well, I'd rather be torrid than torpid.'

'It would be well,' said Mary, 'to praise God for such courage.'

'Is that what *you* praise him for?' we asked her.

'I praise God for Jesus,' Mary said to us: strange talk to be giving the likes of him and me.

We found the finest sleeping nooks, and she could not have rested better if there had been acres of silk; Monk, God-a-mercy, spent his money like a baron. One night in the little darkness he said:

'Look ye're, Mary, tell us why you pray!'

'I pray because of a dream I had.'

'A dream! That's strange, Mary; I could understand a person dreaming because of a prayer she has prayed, but not praying because of a dream she has dreamed.'

'Not even supposing,' I said to him, 'you had dreamed you were praying prayers?'

'If I did,' said he, 'I might pray not to dream such dreams.'

'I pray,' said Mary, 'that my dream may come true.'

[13]

And Monk, he said: 'So you build your life on a prayer and a dream!'

'I do not build my life at all,' said Mary; 'it's my death I am building, in a wonderful world of mountains . . .'

'. . . that can never be climbed,' cried Monk.

'. . . and grand rivers . . .'

'. . . that stand still and do not flow,' says he.

'. . . and bright shining fields . . .'

'. . . that will never come to the reaping,' says he again.

'. . . and if the climbing and the flowing and the reaping are illusions here, they are real in the dreams of God.'

And Monk, he said: 'If God himself is the illusion, Mary, there's little enough reward for a life of that kind, or the death of it either. The recompense for living is Life—not in the future or merely in the present, but life in the past where all our intuitions had their mould, and all our joys their eternal fountain.'

'Yes, yes,' I added to him, 'beauty walks in the track of the mortal world, and her light is behind you.'

She was silent. 'Mary,' said I, 'won't you tell me now that dream of yours?'

'I will not tell you yet, Michael,' said she.

But on a day after that we came to a plain, in it a great mountain; and we went away on to the mountain and commenced to climb. Near the top it was as if part of the cone of the mountain had been blown out by the side and a sweet lake of water left winking in the scoop. We came suddenly upon it; all the cloven cliffs that hung round three sides of the lake were of white marble, blazing with a lustre that crashed upon our eyes; the floor of the lake, easy to be seen, was of white marble too, and the water was that clear you could see the big black hole in the middle where it bubbled from the abyss. There were beds of heather around us with white quoins of marble, like chapels or shrines, sunk amid them; this, and the great golden plain rolling below, far from us, on every side, almost as far away as the sky. When we came to this place Monk touched my arm; we both looked at Mary, walking beside the lake like a person who knew well the marvel that *we* were but just seeing. She was speaking strange words—we could not understand.

'Let us leave her to herself awhile,' said Monk.

And we climbed round behind the white cliffs until we left each other. I went back alone and

[15]

found her lying in the heather beside a stone shaped like an altar, sleeping. I knelt down beside her with a love in my heart that was greater than the mere life beating in it. She lay very still and beautiful, and I put into her hand a sprig of the red rowan which I had found. I watched the wind just hoisting the strands of her hair that was twisted in the heather.

The glister was gone from the cliffs, they were softly white like magnolia flowers; the lake water splashed its little words in the quarries. Her lips were red as the rowan buds, the balm of lilies was in the touch of them.

She opened her eyes on me kneeling beside her.

'Mary,' said I, 'I will tell you what I'm thinking. There is a great doubt in my mind, Mary, and I'm in fear that you'll be gone from me.'

For answer she drew me down to her side until my face was resting against her heart; I could hear its little thunder in her breast. And I leaned up until I was looking deeply in her eyes.

'You are like the dreaming dawn,' I said, 'beautiful and silent. You're the daughter of all the dawns that ever were, and I'd perish if you'd be gone from me.'

'It's beautiful to be in the world with you,

Michael, and to feel your strength about me.'

'It's lonely to be in the world with you, Mary, and no hope in my heart, but doubt filling it.'

'I will bring you into my heaven, Michael.'

'Mary, it's in a little thicket of cedar I would sit with you, hearing the wild bee's hymn; beautiful grapes I would give you, and apples rich as the moon.'

We were silent for awhile and then she told me what I have written here of her own fine words as I remember them. We were sitting against the white altar stone, the sun was setting; there was one great gulf of brightness in the west of the sky, and pieces of fiery cloud, little flukes of flame shaped like fishes, swimming there. In the hinder part of the sky a great bush-tailed animal had sprung into its dying fields, a purple fox.

'I dreamed,' said Mary, 'that I was in marriage with a carpenter. His name was Joseph and he was older than I by many years. He left me at the marriage and went away to Liverpool; there was a great strike on in that place, but what he was to do there or why he was gone I do not know. It was at Easter, and when I woke in my bed on the first morning there was bright wind blowing in the curtains, and sun upon the bed linen. Some cattle were lowing and I heard the very first cuckoo of the year. I can remember the round looking-glass with a brass frame upon the table, and the queer little alabaster jar of scented oil. There was a picture of some cranes flying on the wall, and a china figure of a man called O'Connell on the shelf above the fireplace. My white veil was blown from its hook down on the floor, and it was strewed over with daffodils I had carried to my marriage.

'And at that a figure was in the room—I don't know how—he just came, dressed in strange clothes, a dark handsome young man with black long hair and smiling eyes, full of every grace, and I loved him on the moment. But he took up some of my daffodils only—and vanished. Then I remember getting up, and after breakfast I walked about the fields very happy. There was a letter at the post office from my husband: I took it home and dropped it into the fire unopened. I put the little house into its order and set the daffodils in a bowl close upon the bedroom window. And at night in the darkness, when I could not see him, the dark man came to my bed, but was gone before the morning, taking more of my daffodils with him. And this happened night upon night until all my flowers were gone, and then he came no more.

'It was a long time before my husband came home from Liverpool, but he came at last and we lived very happily until Christmas, when I had a little child.'

'And *did* you have a child?' I asked her.

'No,' she said, 'this was all my dream. Michael, O Michael, you are like that lover of the darkness.'

And just then Monk came back among us roaring for food.

I gave him the bag I had carried and he helped himself.

'I do not feel the need of it,' said Mary.

'I do not feel the need of it,' said I.

When he had told us his tales and the darkness was come we went to rest among the heather.

The wild stars were flowing over the sky, for it was the time of the year when they do fall. Three of them dropped together into the plain near the foot of the mountain, but I lay with the bride of dreams in my arms, and if the lake and the mountain itself had been heaped with immortal stars I would not have stirred. Yet in the morning when I awoke I was alone. There was a new sprig of the rowan in my hand; the grand sun was warm on the rocks and the heather. I stood up and could hear a few birds in the thickets below, little showers of faint music. Mary and Monk were conversing on a ridge under the bank of the lake. I went to them, and Monk touched my arm again as if to give me a warning, but I had no eyes for him, Mary was speaking and pointing.

'Do you see, Michael, that green place at the foot of the mountain?'

'I do, I see a fine green ring.'

'Do you see what is in it?'

'Nothing is in it,' I said, and indeed it was a bare open spot in the ring of a fence, a green slant in the stubbles.

She stared at me with strangely troubled eyes.

'It's a little green terrace, a little sacred terrace; do you not see what is on it?' she asked of Monk.

'There is nothing in it, Mary, but maybe a hare.'

'O look again,' she cried out quickly. 'Michael, there are three golden crosses there, the crosses of Calvary, only they are empty now!'

'There are no crosses there?' I said to Monk.

'There are no crosses there,' he said.

I turned to the girl; she took me in her arms and I shall feel her cold cold lips till the fall of doom.

'Michael, dear, it has been so beautiful. . . .'

She seemed to be making a little farewell and growing vague like a ghost would be.

'O lovely lovely jewel of the world, my heart is losing you! . . . Monk! Monk!' I screamed, but he could not help us. She was gone in a twink, and left me and Monk very lonely in the world.

DUSKY RUTH

At the close of an April day, chilly and wet, the traveller came to a country town. In the Cotswolds, though the towns are small and sweet and the inns snug, the general habit of the land is bleak and bare. He had newly come upon upland roads so void of human affairs, so lonely, that they might have been made for some forgotten uses by departed men, and left to the unwitting passage of such strangers as himself. Even the unending walls, built of old rough laminated rock, that detailed the far-spreading fields, had grown very old again in their courses; there were dabs of darkness, buttons of moss, and fossils on every stone. He had passed a few neighbourhoods, sometimes at the crook of a stream, or at the cross of debouching roads, where old habitations, their gangrenated thatch riddled with bird-holes, had not been so much erected as just spattered about the places. Beyond these signs an odd lark or blackbird, the ruckle of partridges, or the nifty gallop of a hare, had been the only mitigation of the living loneliness that was almost as

profound by day as by night. But the traveller had
a care for such times and places. There are men
who love to gaze with the mind at things that can
never be seen, feel at least the throb of a beauty
that will never be known, and hear over immense
bleak reaches the echo of that which is no celestial
music, but only their own hearts' vain cries; and
though his garments clung to him like clay it was
with deliberate questing step that the traveller trod
the single street of the town, and at last entered the
inn, shuffling his shoes in the doorway for a moment
and striking the raindrops from his hat. Then he
turned into a small smoking-room. Leather-lined
benches, much worn, were fixed to the wall under
the window and in other odd corners and nooks
behind mahogany tables. One wall was furnished
with all the congenial gear of a bar, but without
any intervening counter. Opposite a bright fire was
burning, and a neatly-dressed young woman sat
before it in a Windsor chair, staring at the flames.
There was no other inmate of the room, and as he
entered the girl rose up and greeted him. He found
that he could be accommodated for the night, and
in a few moments his hat and scarf were removed
and placed inside the fender, his wet overcoat was
taken to the kitchen, the landlord, an old fellow,

was lending him a roomy pair of slippers, and a maid was setting supper in an adjoining room.

He sat while this was doing and talked to the barmaid. She had a beautiful, but rather mournful, face as it was lit by the firelight, and when her glance was turned away from it her eyes had a piercing brightness. Friendly and well-spoken as she was, the melancholy in her aspect was noticeable—perhaps it was the dim room, or the wet day, or the long hours ministering a multitude of cocktails to thirsty gallantry.

When he went to his supper he found cheering food and drink, with pleasant garniture of silver and mahogany. There were no other visitors, he was to be alone; blinds were drawn, lamps lit, and the fire at his back was comforting. So he sat long about his meal until a white-faced maid came to clear the table, discoursing to him of country things as she busied about the room. It was a long narrow room, with a sideboard and the door at one end and the fireplace at the other. A bookshelf, almost devoid of books, contained a number of plates; the long wall that faced the windows was almost destitute of pictures, but there were hung upon it, for some inscrutable but doubtless sufficient reason, many dish-covers, solidly

[24]

shaped, of the kind held in such mysterious regard
and known as 'willow pattern'; one was even hung
upon the face of a map. Two musty prints were
mixed with them, presentments of horses having
a stilted extravagant physique and bestridden by
images of inhuman and incommunicable dignity,
clothed in whiskers, coloured jackets and tight
white breeches.

He took down the books from the shelf, but his
interest was speedily exhausted, and the almanacs,
the county directory, and various guide-books were
exchanged for the *Cotswold Chronicle*. With this,
having drawn the deep chair to the hearth, he
whiled away the time. The newspaper amused him
with its advertisements of stock shows, farm
auctions, travelling quacks and conjurers, and there
was a lengthy account of the execution of a local
felon, one Timothy Bridger, who had murdered an
infant in some shameful circumstances. This
dazzling crescendo proved rather trying to the
traveller; he threw down the paper.

The town was all quiet as the hills, and he could
hear no sounds in the house. He got up and went
across the hall to the smoke-room. The door was
shut, but there was light within, and he entered.
The girl sat there much as he had seen her on his

B—AE   [25]

arrival, still alone, with feet in fender. He shut
the door behind him, sat down, and crossing his
legs, puffed at his pipe, admired the snug little
room and the pretty figure of the girl, which he
could do without embarrassment as her meditative
head, slightly bowed, was turned away from him.
He could see something of her, too, in the mirror
at the bar, which repeated also the agreeable
contours of bottles of coloured wines and rich
liqueurs—so entrancing in form and aspect that
they seemed destined to charming histories, even
in disuse—and those of familiar outline containing
mere spirits or small beer, for which are reserved
the harsher destinies of base oils, horse medicines,
disinfectants, and cold tea. There were coloured
glasses for bitter wines, white glasses for sweet, a
tiny leaden sink beneath them, and the four black
handles of the beer engine.

The girl wore a light blouse of silk, a short skirt
of black velvet, and a pair of very thin silk stock-
ings that showed the flesh of instep and shin so
plainly that he could see they were reddened by
the warmth of the fire. She had on a pair of dainty
cloth shoes with high heels, but what was wonderful about her was the heap of rich black hair piled
at the back of her head and shadowing the dusky

[26]

neck. He sat puffing his pipe and letting the loud tick of the clock fill the quiet room. She did not stir and he could move no muscle. It was as if he had been willed to come there and wait silently. That, he felt now, had been his desire all the evening; and here, in her presence, he was more strangely stirred than by any event he could remember.

In youth he had viewed women as futile pitiable things that grew long hair, wore stays and garters, and prayed incomprehensible prayers. Viewing them in the stalls of the theatre from his vantage-point in the gallery, he always disliked the articulation of their naked shoulders. But still, there was a god in the sky, a god with flowing hair and exquisite eyes, whose one stride with an ardour grandly rendered took him across the whole round hemisphere to which his buoyant limbs were bound like spokes to the eternal rim and axle, his bright hair burning in the pity of the sunsets and tossing in the anger of the dawns.

Master traveller had indeed come into this room to be with this woman: she as surely desired him, and for all its accidental occasion it was as if he, walking the ways of the world, had suddenly come upon . . . what so imaginable with all permitted reverence as, well, just a shrine; and he, admirably humble, bowed the instant head.

Were there no other people within? The clock indicated a few minutes to nine. He sat on, still as stone, and the woman might have been of wax for all the movement or sound she made. There was allurement in the air between them; he had forborne his smoking, the pipe grew cold between his teeth. He waited for a look from her, a movement to break the trance of silence. No footfall in street or house, no voice in the inn, but the clock beating away as if pronouncing a doom. Suddenly it rasped out nine large notes, a bell in the town repeated them dolefully, and a cuckoo no further than the kitchen mocked them with three times three. After that came the weak steps of the old landlord along the hall, the slam of doors, the clatter of lock and bolt, and then the silence returning unendurably upon them.

He arose and stood behind her; he touched the black hair. She made no movement or sign. He pulled out two or three combs, and dropping them into her lap let the whole mass tumble about his hands. It had a curious harsh touch in the unravelling, but was so full and shining; black as a rook's wings it was. He slid his palms through it.

[28]

His fingers searched it and fought with its fine strangeness; into his mind there travelled a serious thought, stilling his wayward fancy—this was no wayward fancy, but a rite accomplishing itself! (*Run, run, silly man, y'are lost!*) But having got so far he burnt his boats, leaned over, and drew her face back to him. And at that, seizing his wrists, she gave him back ardour for ardour, pressing his hands to her bosom, while the kiss was sealed and sealed again. Then she sprang up and picking his hat and scarf from the fender said:

'I have been drying them for you, but the hat has shrunk a bit, I'm sure—I tried it on.'

He took them from her, and put them behind him; he leaned lightly back upon the table, holding it with both his hands behind him; he could not speak.

'Aren't you going to thank me for drying them?' she asked, picking her combs from the rug and re-pinning her hair.

'I wonder why we did that?' he asked shamedly.

'It is what I'm thinking too,' she said.

'You were so beautiful about . . . about it, you know.'

She made no rejoinder, but continued to bind her hair, looking brightly at him under her brows.

When she had finished she went close to him.

'Will that do?'

'I'll take it down again.'

'No, no, the old man or the old woman will be coming in.'

'What of that?' he said, taking her into his arms. 'Tell me your name.'

She shook her head, but she returned his kisses and stroked his hair and shoulders with beautifully melting gestures.

'What is your name, I want to call you by your name?' he said. 'I can't keep calling you Lovely Woman, Lovely Woman.'

Again she shook her head and was dumb.

'I'll call you Ruth then, Dusky Ruth, Ruth of the black, beautiful hair.'

'That is a nice-sounding name—I knew a deaf and dumb girl named Ruth; she went to Nottingham and married an organ-grinder—but I should like it for my name.'

'Then I give it to you.'

'Mine is so ugly.'

'What is it?'

Again the shaken head and the burning caress.

'Then you shall be Ruth; will you keep that name?'

'Yes, if you give me the name I will keep it for you.'

Time had indeed taken them by the forelock, and they looked upon a ruddled world.

'I stake my one talent,' he said jestingly, 'and behold it returns me fortyfold; I feel like the boy who catches three mice with one piece of cheese.'

At ten o'clock the girl said:

'I must go and see how *they* are getting on,' and she went to the door.

'Are we keeping them up?'

She nodded.

'Are you tired?'

'No, I am not tired.'

She looked at him doubtfully.

'We ought not to stay in here; go into the coffee-room and I'll come there in a few minutes.

'Right,' he whispered gaily, 'we'll sit up all night.'

She stood at the door for him to pass out, and he crossed the hall to the other room. It was in darkness except for the flash of the fire. Standing at the hearth he lit a match for the lamp, but paused at the globe; then he extinguished the match.

'No, it's better to sit in the firelight.'

He heard voices at the other end of the house

[31]

that seemed to have a chiding note in them.

'Lord,' he thought, 'she is getting into a row?'

Then her steps came echoing over the stone floors of the hall; she opened the door and stood there with a lighted candle in her hand; he stood at the other end of the room, smiling.

'Good night,' she said.

'Oh no, no! come along,' he protested, but not moving from the hearth.

'Got to go to bed,' she answered.

'Are they angry with you?'

'No.'

'Well, then, come over here and sit down.'

'Got to go to bed,' she said again, but she had meanwhile put her candlestick upon the little sideboard and was trimming the wick with a burnt match.

'Oh, come along, just half an hour,' he protested. She did not answer but went on prodding the wick of the candle.

'Ten minutes, then,' he said, still not going towards her.

'Five minutes,' he begged.

She shook her head, and picking up the candlestick turned to the door. He did not move, he just called her name: 'Ruth!'

She came back then, put down the candlestick and tiptoed across the room until he met her. The bliss of the embrace was so poignant that he was almost glad when she stood up again and said with affected steadiness, though he heard the tremor in her voice:

'I must get you your candle.'

She brought one from the hall, set it on the table in front of him, and struck the match.

'What is my number?' he asked.

'Number six room,' she answered, prodding the wick vaguely with her match, while a slip of white wax dropped over the shoulder of the new candle. 'Number six . . . next to mine.'

The match burnt out; she said abruptly 'Good night,' took up her own candle and left him there.

In a few moments he ascended the stairs and went into his room. He fastened the door, removed his coat, collar, and slippers, but the rack of passion had seized him and he moved about with no inclination to sleep. He sat down, but there was no medium of distraction. He tried to read the newspaper which he had carried up with him, and without realizing a single phrase, he forced himself to read again the whole account of the execution of the miscreant Bridger. When he had finished this he carefully folded the paper and stood up, listening. He went to the parting wall and tapped thereon with his finger-tips. He waited half a minute, one minute, two minutes; there was no answering sign. He tapped again, more loudly, with his knuckles, but there was no response, and he tapped many times. He opened his door as noiselessly as possible; along the dark passage there were slips of light under the other doors, the one next his own, and the one beyond that. He stood in the corridor listening to the rumble of old voices in the farther room, the old man and his wife going to their rest. Holding his breath fearfully, he stepped to *her* door and tapped gently upon it. There was no answer, but he could somehow divine her awareness of him; he tapped again; she moved to the door and whispered 'No, no, go away.' He turned the handle, the door was locked.

'Let me in,' he pleaded. He knew she was standing there an inch or two beyond him.

'Hush,' she called softly. 'Go away, the old woman has ears like a fox.'

He stood silent for a moment.

'Unlock it,' he urged; but he got no further reply, and feeling foolish and baffled he moved back

[34]

to his own room, cast his clothes from him, doused the candle and crept into the bed with soul as wild as a storm-swept forest, his heart beating a vagrant summons. The room filled with strange heat, there was no composure for mind or limb, nothing but flaming visions and furious embraces.

'Morality . . . what is it but agreement with your own soul?'

So he lay for two hours—the clocks chimed twelve—listening with foolish persistency for *her* step along the corridor, fancying every light sound —and the night was full of them—was her hand upon the door.

Suddenly,—and then it seemed as if his very heart would abash the house with its thunder—he could hear distinctly some one knocking on the wall. He got quickly from his bed and stood at the door, listening. Again the knocking was heard, and having half clothed himself he crept into the passage, which was now in utter darkness, trailing his hand along the wall until he felt her door; it was standing open. He entered her room and closed the door behind him. There was not the faintest gleam of light, he could see nothing. He whispered 'Ruth!' and she was standing there. She touched him, but not speaking. He put out his hands, and they met round her neck; her hair was flowing in its great wave about her; he put his lips to her face and found that her eyes were streaming with tears, salt and strange and disturbing. In the close darkness he put his arms about her with no thought but to comfort her; one hand had plunged through the long harsh tresses and the other across her hips before he realized that she was ungowned; then he was aware of the softness of her breasts and the cold naked sleekness of her shoulders. But she was crying there, crying silently with great tears, her strange sorrow stifling his desire.

'Ruth, Ruth, my beautiful dear!' he murmured soothingly. He felt for the bed with one hand, and turning back the quilt and sheets he lifted her in as easily as a mother does her child, replaced the bedding, and, in his clothes, he lay stretched beside her comforting her. They lay so, innocent as children, for an hour, when she seemed to have gone to sleep. He rose then and went silently to his room, full of weariness.

In the morning he breakfasted without seeing her, but as he had business in the world that gave him just an hour longer at the inn before he left it for good and all, he went into the smoke-room and found her. She greeted him with curious gaze, but merrily enough, for there were other men there now, farmers, a butcher, a registrar, an old, old man. The hour passed, but not these men, and at length he donned his coat, took up his stick, and said good-bye. Her shining glances followed him to the door, and from the window as far as they could view him.

WEEP NOT MY WANTON

Air and light on Sack Down at summer sunset were soft as ointment and sweet as milk; at least, that is the notion the down might give to a mind that bloomed within its calm horizons, some happy victim of romance it might be, watching the silken barley moving in its lower fields with the slow movement of summer sea, reaching no harbour, having no end. The toilers had mostly given over; their ploughs and harrows were left to the abandoned fields; they had taken their wages and gone, or were going, home; but at the crown of the hill a black barn stood by the roadside, and in its yard, amid sounds of anguish, a score of young boar pigs were being gelded by two brown lads and a gipsy fellow. Not half a mile of distance here could enclose you the compass of their cries. If a man desired peace he would step fast down the hill towards Arwall with finger in ear until he came to quiet at a bank overlooking slopes of barley, and could perceive the fogs of June being born in the standing grass beyond.

Four figures, a labourer and his family, travelled slowly up the road proceeding across the hill, a sound mingling dully with their steps—the voice of the man. You could not tell if it were noise of voice or of footsteps that first came into your ear, but it could be defined on their advance as the voice of a man upbraiding his little son.

'You're a naughty, naughty—you're a vurry, *vurry* naughty boy! Oi can't think what's comen tyeh!'

The father towered above the tiny figure shuffling under his elbow, and kept his eyes stupidly fixed upon him. He saw a thin boy, a spare boy, a very shrunken boy of seven or eight years, crying quietly. He let no grief out of his lips, but his white face was streaming with dirty tears. He wore a man's cap, an unclean sailor jacket, large knickerbockers that made a mockery of his lean joints, a pair of women's button boots, and he looked straight ahead.

'The idear! To go and lose a sixpence like that then! Where d'ye think yer'll land yerself, ay? Wher'd I be if I kept on losing sixpences, ay? A creature like you, ay?' and lifting his heavy hand the man struck the boy a blow behind with shock enough to disturb a heifer. They went on, the

[39]

child with sobs that you could feel rather than hear. As they passed the black barn the gipsy bawled encouragingly: 'Selp me, father, that's a good 'un, wallop his trousers!'

But the man ignored him, as he ignored the yell of the pig and the voice of the lark rioting above them all; he continued his litany:

'You're a naughty, naughty *boy*, an' I dunno what's comen tyeh!'

The woman, a poor slip of a woman she was, walked behind them with a smaller child: she seemed to have no desire to shield the boy or to placate the man. She did not seem to notice them, and led the toddling babe, to whom she gabbled, some paces in the rear of the man of anger. He was a great figure with a bronzed face; his trousers were tied at the knee, his wicker bag was slung over his shoulder. With his free and massive hand he held the hand of the boy. He was slightly drunk, and walked with his legs somewhat wide, at the beginning of each stride lifting his heel higher than was required, and at the end of it placing his foot firmly but obliquely inwards. There were two bright medals on the breast of his waistcoat, presumably for valour; he was perhaps a man who would stand upon his rights and his dignities, such

[40]

as they were—but then he was drunk. His language, oddly unprofane, gave a subtle and mean point to his decline from the heroic standard. He only ceased his complaining to gaze swayingly at the boy; then he struck him. The boy, crying quietly, made no effort to avoid or resist him.

'You understand me, you bad boy! As long as you're with me you got to come under collar. And wher'll you be next I *dunno*, a bad creature like you, ay! An' then to turn roun' an' answer me! *I dunno!* I dunno *what's* comen tyeh. Ye know ye lost that sixpence through glammering about. Wher d'ye lose it, ay? Wher d'ye lose it, ay?'

At these questions he seized the boy by the neck and shook him as a child does a bottle of water. The baby behind them was taken with little gusts of laughter at the sight, and the woman cooed back playfully at her.

'George, George!' yelled the woman.

The man turned round.

'Look after Annie!' she yelled again.

'What's up?' he called.

Her only answer was a giggle of laughter as she disappeared behind a hedge. The child toddled up to its father and took his hand, while the quiet boy took her other hand with relief. She laughed up into their faces, and the man resumed his homily.

'He's a bad, bad boy. He's a vurry *naughty* bad boy!'

By and by the woman came shuffling after them; the boy looked furtively around and dropped his sister's hand.

'Carm on, my beauty!' cried the man, lifting the girl to his shoulder. 'He's a bad boy; you 'ave a ride on your daddy.' They went on alone, and the woman joined the boy. He looked up at her with a sad face.

'O, my Christ, Johnny!' she said, putting her arms round the boy, 'what's 'e bin doin' to yeh? Yer face is all blood!'

'It's only me nose, mother. Here,' he whispered, 'here's the tanner.'

They went together down the hill towards the inn, which had already a light in its windows. The screams from the barn had ceased, and a cart passed them full of young pigs, bloody and subdued. The hill began to resume its old dominion of soft sounds. It was nearly nine o'clock, and one anxious farmer still made hay although, on this side of the down, day had declined, and with a greyness that came not from the sky, but crept up from the world. From the quiet hill, as the last skein of cocks was carted to the stack, you could hear dimly men's voices and the rattle of their gear.

PIFFINGCAP

PIFFINGCAP had the cup from an old friend, a queer-minded man. He had given it to him just before he had gone out of this continent, not for the first but for the last time—a cup of lead with an inscription upon it in decent letters but strange words.

'Here, Elmer,' said his old friend to the barber of Bagwood, 'have this—there's the doom of half a million beards in it!'

Piffingcap laughed, but without any joy, for his heart was heavy to lose his friend.

'There is in it too,' continued Grafton, offering the pot and tapping it with his forefinger, 'a true test of virtue—a rare thing, as you know, in these parts. Secondly, there is in it a choice of fortunes; and thirdly, it may be, a triple calamity and—and—and very serious, you know, but there you are.' He gave it into the barber's hand with a slight sigh. While his friend duly admired the dull gift the traveller picked up his walking stick and winked at himself in the mirror.

And Elmer Piffingcap, the barber of Bagwood, took his friend's cup, set it in a conspicuous place upon the shelf of his shop, and bade that friend good-bye, a little knot rolling into his lungs as they shook their two hands together.

'It is true, then,' said he, staring at the shining baldness of his friend who stood with hat and stick in hand—for as Piffingcap dared not look into his friend's eyes, the gleam of the skull took his gaze, as a bright thing will seize the mind of a gnat—'it is true, then, I shall see you no more?'

'No more again,' said the wanderer affably, replacing his hat—disliking that pliant will-less stare of the barber's mournful eyes. This wandering man had a heart full of bravery though he could not walk with pride, for the corns and bunkles he suffered would have crippled a creature of four feet, leave alone two. But—would you believe it—he was going now to walk himself for all his days round and round the world. O, he was such a man as could put a deceit upon the slyest, with his tall hat and his jokes, living as easy as a bird in the softness and sweetness of the year.

'And if it rains, it rains,' he declared to Polly, 'and I squat like a hare in the hedge and keep the blessed bones of me dry and my feet warm—it's

[45]

not three weeks since it happened to me; my neck as damp as the inside of an onion, and my curly locks caught in blackberry bushes—stint your laughing, Polly!—the end of my nose as cold as a piece of dead pork, and the place very inconvenient with its sharp thorns and nettles—and no dock-leaf left in the whole parish. But there was young barley wagging in the field, and clover to be smelling, and rooks to be watching, and doves, and the rain heaving its long sigh in the greyness—I declare to my God it was a fine handsome day I had that day, Polly!'

In the winter he would be sleeping in decent nooks, eating his food in quiet inns, drying his coat at the forge; and so he goes now into the corners of the world—the little husky fat man, with large spectacles and fox coloured beard and tough boots that had slits and gouts in them—gone seeking the feathers out of Priam's peacock. And let him go; we take no more concern of him or his shining skull or his tra-la-la in the highways.

The barber, who had a romantic drift of mind, went into his saloon, and taking up the two cracked china lather mugs he flung them from the open window into his back garden, putting the fear of some evil into the mind of his drowsy cat, and a

[46]

great anticipation in the brains of his two dusty
hens, who were lurking there for anything that
could be devoured. Mr. Piffingcap placed the pot
made of lead upon his convenient shelf, laid
therein his brush, lit the small gas stove under the
copper urn, and when Polly, the child from the
dairy, arrived with her small can for the barber's
large jug she found him engaged in shaving the chin
of Timmy James the butcher, what time Mr. James
was engaged in a somewhat stilted conversation
with Gregory Barnes about the carnal women of
Bagwood.

Polly was a little lean girl, eight or nine years
old, with a face that was soft and rosy and fresh
as the bud of gum on the black branches of the
orchard. She wore a pretty dimity frock and had
gay flowers in her hat. This was her last house of
call, and, sitting down to watch Mr. Piffingcap,
the town's one barber, shaving friends and enemies
alike, she would be the butt of their agreeable
chaff because of her pleasant country jargon—as
rich as nutmeg in a homely cake—or her yellow
scattered hair, or her sweet eyes that were soft as
remembered twilight.

'Your razor is roaring, Mr. Piffingcap!'—peep-
ing round the chair at him. 'Oh, it's that Mr.

James!' she would say in pretended surprise. Mr. James had a gruff beard, and the act of removing it occasioned a noise resembling that of her mother scraping the new potatoes.

'What have you got this pot for?' she chattered; 'I don't like it, it's ugly.'

'Don't say that now,' said Mr. Piffingcap, pausing with his hand on the butcher's throttle, 'it was Mr. Grafton's parting gift to me; I shall never see him again, nor will you neither; he's gone round the world for evermore this time!'

'Oh!' gurgled the child in a manner that hung between pain and delight, 'has he gone to Rinjig-offer land?'

'Gone where?' roared Timothy James, lifting his large red neck from the rest.

'He's told me all about it,' said the child, ignoring him.

'Well, he's not gone there,' interrupted the barber.

And the child continued, 'It's where the doves and the partridges are so fat that they break down the branches of the trees where they roost . . .'

'Garn with yer!' said Mr. James.

'. . . and the hares are as big as foxes . . .'

'God-a-mercy!' said Mr. James.

'. . . yes, and a fox was big and brown and white like a skew-bald donkey—he! he! he! And, oo yes,' continued Polly, shrilling with excitement, 'there was a king badger as would stop your eyes from winking if you met him walking in the dawn!'

'Lord, what should the man be doing telling you them lies,' ejaculated Timothy, now wiping his chin on the napkin. 'Did he give you that cup, Piff?'

'Yes,' replied the barber, 'and if what he says is true there's a power o' miracle in it.'

The butcher surveyed it cautiously and read the inscription:

NE SAMBRA DIVORNAK

'That's a bit o' Roosian, I should say,' he remarked as he and Gregory left the saloon.

Polly picked up her empty can and looked at Mr. P.

'Won't he come back no more?'

'No, Polly, my pigeon, he won't come back.'

'Didn't he like us?' asked the child.

The barber stood dumb before her bright searching eyes.

'He was better than my father,' said the child, 'or me uncle, or the schoolmaster.'

'He's the goodest man alive, Polly,' said Mr. P.

'Didn't he like us?' again she asked; and as Mr.

[49]

P. could only look vaguely about the room she went out and closed the latch of the door very softly behind her.

In the succeeding days the barber lathered and cut or sat smoking meditatively in his saloon; the doom began to work its will, and business, which for a quarter of a century had flourished like a plant, as indeed it was, of constant and assured growth, suddenly declined. On weekdays the barber cleaned up the chins of his fellow townsmen alone, but on Sunday mornings he would seek the aid of a neighbour, a youngster whom he called Charleyboy, when four men would be seated at one time upon his shaving-chairs, towel upon breast and neck bared for the sacrifice, while Charleyboy dabbed and pounded their crops into foam. Mr. Piffingcap would follow him, plying his weapon like the genius he was, while Charleyboy again in turn followed *him*, drying with linen, cooling with rhum, or soothing with splendid unguent. 'Next gent, please!' he would cry out, and the last short man would rise and turn away, dabbing his right hand into the depths of his breeches pocket and elevating that with his left before producing the customary tribute.

But the genius of Piffingcap and the neat hand

of Charley languished in distress. There was no gradual cessation, the thing completely stopped, and Piffingcap did not realize until too late, until, indeed, the truth of it was current in the little town everywhere but in his own shop, that the beards once shaven by him out of Grafton's pot grew no more in Bagwood; and there came the space of a week or so when not a soul entered the saloon but two schoolboys for the cutting of hair, and a little housemaid for a fringe net.

Then he knew, and one day, having sat in the place the whole morning like a beleaguered rat, with ruin and damnation a hand's-breadth only from him, he rushed from his shop across to the hardware merchant's and bought two white china mugs, delicately lined with gold and embossed with vague lumps, and took them back to the saloon.

At dinner-time he put the cup of lead into his coat pocket and walked down the street in an anxious kind of way until he came to the bridge at the end of the town. It was an angular stone bridge, crossing a deep and leisurely flowing river, along whose parapet boys had dared a million times, wearing smooth, with their adventuring feet, its soft yellow stone. He stared at the water and saw the shining flank of a tench as it turned over. All beyond the bridge were meads thick with ripe unmown grass and sweet with scabious bloom. But the barber's mind was harsh with the rancour of noon heats and the misfortunes of life. He stood with one hand resting upon the hot stone and one upon the heavy evil thing in his pocket. The bridge was deserted at this hour, its little traffic having paused for the meal. He took, at length, the cup from his pocket, and whispered to himself 'God forgive you, Grafton,' he let it fall from his fingers into the water; then he walked sharply home to his three daughters and told them what he had done.

'You poor loon!' said Bersa.

'O man! man!' moaned Grue.

'You're the ruin of us all!' cried Mavie.

Three fine women were Grue and Mavie and Bersa, in spite of the clamour of the outlandish Piffingcap names, and their father had respect for them and admired their handsomeness. But they had for their father, all three of them, the principal filial emotion of compassion, and they showed that his action had been a foolish action, that there were other towns in the world besides Bagwood, and that thousands and millions of men would pay a good price to be quit of a beard, and be shaved from a pot that would complete the destruction of all the unwanted hairiness of the world. And they were very angry with him.

'Let us go and see to it . . . what is to be done now . . . bring us to the place, father!'

He took them down to the river, and when they peered over the side of the bridge they could see the pot lying half sunk in some white sand in more than a fathom of water.

'Let us instruct the waterman,' they said, 'he will secure it for us.'

In the afternoon Grue met the waterman, who was a sly young fellow, and she instructed him, but at teatime word was brought to Piffingcap that the young waterman was fallen into the river and drowned. Then there was grief in his mind, for he remembered the calamity which Grafton had foretold, and he was for giving up all notions of retaking the cup; but his daughter Bersa went in a few days to a man who was an angler and instructed him; and he took a crooked pole and leaned over the bridge to probe for the cup. In the afternoon word was brought to Piffingcap that the parapet had given way, and the young angler in falling through had dashed out his brains on the abutment of the bridge. And the young gaffer whom Mavie instructed was took of a sunstroke and died on the bank.

The barber was in great grief at these calamities; he had tremors of guilt in his mind, no money in his coffers, and the chins of the Bagwood men were still as smooth as children's; but it came to him one day that he need not fear any more calamities, and that a thing which had so much tricks in it should perhaps be cured by trickery.

'I will go,' he said, 'to the Widow Buckland and ask her to assist me.'

The Widow Buckland was a wild strange woman who lived on a heath a few miles away from Bagwood; so he went over one very hot day to the Widow and found her cottage in the corner of the heath. There was a caravan beside the cottage— it was a red caravan with yellow wheels. A blackbird hung in a wicker cage at the door, and on the side of the roof board was painted

AGLAURA BUCKLAND

FEATS & GALIAS ATENDED

There was nobody in the caravan, so he knocked at the cottage door; the Widow Buckland led him into her dim little parlour.

'It 'ull cost you half a James!' says she when Mr. Piffingcap had given her his requirements.

'Half a what?' cried he.

'You are *not*,' said the gipsy, 'a man of a mean heart, are you?' She said it very persuasively, and he felt he could not annoy her for she was a very large woman with sharp glances.

'No,' said Piffingcap.

'And you'll believe what I'm telling you, won't you?'

'Yes,' said Piffingcap.

'It 'ull maybe some time before my words come true, but come true they will, I can take *my* oath.'

'Yes,' again said Piffingcap.

'George!' she bawled to some one from the doorway, 'wher'd yer put my box?'

There was an indistinct reply, but she bawled out again, 'Well, *fetch* it off the rabbit hutch.'

'And a man like you,' she continued, turning again to the barber, 'doesn't think twice about half a sovereign, and me putting you in the way of what you want to know, *I'm* sure.'

And Piffingcap mumbled dubiously 'No,' producing with difficulty some shillings, some coppers, and a postal order for one and threepence which a credulous customer had that morning sent him for a bottle of hairwash.

'Let's look at your 'and,' she said; taking it, she reflected gravely:

[55]

'You're a man that's 'ad your share 'o trouble, ain't you?'

Piffingcap bowed meekly.

'And you've 'ad your 'appy days, ain't you?'

A nod.

'Well listen to me; you've got more fortune in store for you if you know how to pluck it . . . you understand my meaning, don't you? . . . than any man in the town this bleedun minute. Right, George,' she exclaimed, turning to a very ugly little hunch-backed fellow—truly he was a mere squint of a man, there was such a little bit of him for so much uncomeliness. The Widow Buckland took the box from the hunchback and, thrusting him out of the room, she shut fast the door and turned the key in the lock. Then she drew up a bit of a table to the window, and taking out of the box a small brass vessel and two bottles she set them before her.

'Sit down there, young feller,' she said, and Piffingcap sat down at the end of the table facing the window. The Widow turned to the window, which was a small square, the only one in the room, and closed over it a shutter. The room was clapped in darkness except for a small ray in the middle of the shutter, coming through a round hole about as large as a guinea. She pulled Mr. Piffingcap's shoulder until the ray was shining on the middle of his forehead; she took up the brass vessel, and holding it in the light of the ray polished it for some time with her forefinger. All her fingers, even her thumbs, were covered with rich sinister rings, but there were no good looks in those fingers for the nails had been munched almost away, and dirty skin hid up the whites. The polished vessel was then placed on the table directly beneath the ray; drops from the two phials were poured into it, a green liquid and a black liquid; mixing together they melted into a pillar of smoke which rose and was seen only as it flowed through the beam of light, twisting and veering and spinning in strange waves.

The Widow Buckland said not a word for a time, but contemplated the twisting shapes as they poured through the ray, breathing heavily all the while or suffering a slight sigh to pass out of her breast. But shortly the smoke played the barber a trick in his nose and heaving up his chin he rent the room with a great sneeze. When he recovered himself she was speaking certain words.

'Fire and water I see and a white virgin's skin. The triple gouts of blood I see and the doom given

over. Fire and water I see and a white virgin's
skin.'

She threw open the shutter, letting in the light;
smoke had ceased to rise, but it filled the parlour
with a sweet smell.

'Well . . .' said Mr. Piffingcap dubiously.

And the Widow Buckland spoke over to him
plainly and slowly, patting his shoulder at each
syllable.

'Fire and water and a white virgin's skin.'

Unlatching the door she thrust him out of the
house into the sunlight. He tramped away across
the heath meditating her words, and coming to
the end of it he sat down in the shade of a bush
by the side of the road, for he felt sure he was
about to capture the full meaning of her words.
But just then he heard a strange voice speaking, and
speaking very vigorously. He looked up and
observed a man on a bicycle, riding along towards
him, talking to himself in a great way.

'He is a political fellow rehearsing a speech,' said
Mr. Piffingcap to himself, 'or perhaps he is some
holy-minded person devising a sermon.'

It was a very bald man and he had a long face
hung with glasses; he had no coat and rode in his
shirt and knickerbockers, with hot thick stock-

ings and white shoes. The barber watched him after he had passed and noted how his knees turned angularly outwards at each upward movement, and how his saddle-bag hung at the bottom of his back like some ironical label.

'Fool!' exclaimed Mr. Piffingcap, rising angrily, for the man's chatter had driven his mind clean away from the Widow Buckland's meaning. But it was only for a short while, and when he got home he called one of his daughters into the saloon.

'My child,' said Piffingcap, 'you know the great trouble which is come on me?' and he told Bersa his difficulty and requested her aid, that is to say: would she go down in the early morning in her skin only and recover the pot?

'Indeed no, father,' said his daughter Bersa, 'it is a very evil thing and I will not do your request.'

'You will not?' says he.

'No!' says she, but it was not in the fear of her getting her death that she refused him.

So he called to another of his daughters.

'My child,' said he, 'you know the great trouble that is come on me?' and he told Mavie his desire and asked for her aid.

'Why, my father,' says she, 'this is a thing which

a black hag has put on us all and I will get my death. I love you as I love my life, father, but I won't do this!'

'You will not?' says he.

'No!' says she, but it was not for fear of her death she refused him.

And he went to his third daughter Grue and tried her with the same thing. 'My child, you know the trouble that's come on me?'

'Oh, will you let me alone!' she says, 'I've a greater trouble on me than your mouldy pot.' And it is true what she said of her trouble, for she was a girl of a loose habit. So the barber said no more to them and went to his bed.

Two days later, it being Saturday, he opened in the morning his saloon and sat down there. And while he read his newspaper in the empty place footsteps scampered into his doorway, and the door itself was pushed open just an inch or two.

'Come in,' he said, rising.

The door opened fully.

'Zennybody here?' whispered Polly, walking in very mysteriously, out of breath, and dressed in a long mackintosh.

'What is the matter, my little one?' he asked, putting his arm around her shoulders, for he had a fondness for her. 'Ach, your hair's all wet, what's the matter?'

The little girl put her hand under the mackintosh and drew out the leaden pot, handing it to the barber and smiling at him with inarticulate but intense happiness. She said not a word as he stared his surprise and joy.

'Why, Polly, my *dear*, how *did* you get it?'

'I dived in and got it.'

'You never . . . you princess . . . you!'

'I just bin and come straight here with it.'

She opened and shut the mackintosh quickly, displaying for a brief glance her little white naked figure with the slightest tremulous crook at the sharp knees.

'Ah, my darling,' exclaimed the enraptured barber, 'and you're shivering with not a rag on you but them shoes . . . run away home, Polly, and get some things on, Polly . . . and . . . Polly, Polly!' as she darted away, 'come back quick, won't you?'

She nodded brightly back at him as she sprang through the doorway. He went to the entrance and watched her taking her twinkling leaps, as bonny as a young foal, along the pavement.

And there came into the barber's mind the notion

that this was all again a piece of fancy tricks; but there was the dark pot, and he examined it. Thoughtfully he took it into his backyard and busied himself there for a while, not telling his daughters of its recovery. When, later, Polly joined him in the garden he had already raised a big fire in an old iron brazier which had lain there.

'Ah, Polly, my dear, I'm overjoyed to get it back, but I dasn't keep it . . . it's a bad thing. Take it in your fingers now, my dear little girl, and just chuck it in that fire. Ah, we must melt the wickedness out of it,' he said, observing her disappointment; 'it's been the death of three men and we dasn't keep it.'

They watched it among the coals until it had begun to perish drop by drop through the grating of the brazier.

Later in the day Mr. Piffingcap drove Polly in a little trap to a neighbouring town to see a circus, and the pair of them had a roaring dinner at the Green Dragon. Next morning when Polly brought the milk to the saloon there were Timmy James and Gregory Barnes being shaved, for beards had grown again in Bagwood.

THE KING OF THE WORLD

ONCE upon a time, yes, in the days of King Sennacherib, a young Assyrian captain, valiant and desirable, but more hapless than either, fleeing in that strange rout of the armies against Judah, was driven into the desert. Daily his company perished from him until he alone, astride a camel, was left searching desperately through a boundless desert for the loved plains of Shinar, sweet with flocks and rich with glittering cities. The desolation of ironic horizons that he could never live to pierce hung hopelessly in remote unattainable distances, endless as the blue sky. The fate of his comrades had left upon him a small pack of figs and wine, but in that uncharted wilderness it was but a pitiable parrying of death's last keen stroke. There was no balm or succour in that empty sky; blue it was as sapphires, but savage with rays that scourged like flaming brass. Earth itself was not less empty, and the loneliness of his days was an increasing bitterness. He was so deeply forgotten of men, and so removed from the savour of life, from his lost country, the men he knew, the women he loved, their temples, their markets and their homes, that it seemed the gods had drawn that sweet and easy world away from his entangled feet.

But at last upon a day he was astonished and cheered by the sight of a black butterfly flickering in the air before him, and towards evening he espied a giant mound lying lonely in the east. He drove his camel to it, but found only a hill of sand whirled up by strange winds of the desert. He cast himself from the camel's back and lay miserably in the dust. His grief was extreme, but in time he tended his tired beast and camped in the shadow of the hill. When he gave himself up to sleep the night covering them was very calm and beautiful, the sky soft and streaming with stars; it seemed to his saddened mind that the desert and the deep earth were indeed dead, and life and love only in that calm enduring sky. But at midnight a storm arose with quickening furies that smote the desert to its unseen limits, and the ten thousand stars were flung into oblivion; winds flashed upon him with a passion more bitter than a million waves, a terror greater than hosts of immediate enemies. They grasped and plunged him into gulfs of darkness, heaped mountains upon him, lashed him with thongs of snakes and scattered him with scimitars of unspeakable fear. His soul was tossed in the void like a crushed star and his body beaten into the dust with no breath left him to bemoan his fate. Nevertheless, by a miracle his soul and body lived on.

It was again day when he recovered, day in the likeness of yesterday, the horizons still infinitely far. Long past noon, the sun had turned in the sky; he was alone. The camel was doubtless buried in the fathoms he himself had escaped, but a surprising wonder greeted his half-blinded eyes; the hill of sand was gone, utterly, blown into the eternal waste of the desert, and in its track stood a strange thing—a shrine. There was a great unroofed pavement of onyx and blue jasper, large enough for the floor of a temple, with many life-sized figures, both men and women, standing upon it all carved in rock and facing, at the sacred end, a giant pillared in black basalt, seven times the height of a man. The sad captain divined at once that this was the lost shrine of Namu-Sarkkon, the dead god of whom tradition spoke in the ancient litanies of his country. He heaved himself painfully from the grave of sand in which he had lain half-buried, and staggering to the pavement, leaned in the shade of one of those figures fronting the dead god. In a little time he recovered and ate some figs which he carried in a leather bag at his hip, and plucked the sand from his eyes and ears and loosened his sandals and gear. Then he bowed himself for a moment before the black immobile idol, knowing that he would tarry here now until he died.

Namu-Sarkkon, the priestless god, had been praised of old time above all for his gifts of joy. Worshippers had gathered from the cities of Assyria at this his only shrine, offering their souls for a gift to him who, in his time and wisdom, granted their desires. But Namu-Sarkkon, like other gods, was a jealous god, and, because the hearts of mankind are vain and destined to betrayal, he turned the bodies of his devotees into rock and kept them pinioned in stone for a hundred years, or for a thousand years, according to the nature of their desires. Then if the consummation were worthy and just, the rock became a living fire, the blood of eternity quickened the limbs, and the god released the body full of youth and joy. But what god lives for ever? Not Namu-Sarkkon. He grew old and forgetful; his oracle was defamed. Stronger gods supplanted him and at last all power departed save only from one of his eyes. That eye possessed the favour of eternity, but only so faintly that the

worshipper when released from his trap of stone
lived at the longest but a day, some said even but
an hour. None could then be found to exchange
the endurances of the world for so brief a happiness.
His worship ceased, Namu-Sarkkon was dead, and
the remote shrine being lost to man's heart was
lost to man's eyes. Even the tradition of its time
and place had become a mere fantasy, but the
whirlwinds of uncounted years sowing their sands
about the shrine had left it blameless and unperish-
able, if impotent.

Recollecting this, the soldier gazed long at the
dead idol. Its smooth, huge bulk, carved wonder-
fully, was still without blemish and utterly cleansed
of the sand. The strange squat body with the
benign face stood on stout legs, one advanced as
if about to stride forward to the worshipper, and
one arm outstretched offered the sacred symbol.
Then in a moment the Assyrian's heart leaped within
him; he had been staring at the mild eyes of the god
—surely there was a movement in one of the eyes!
He stood erect, trembling, then flung himself
prostrate before Namu-Sarkkon, the living god!
He lay long, waiting for his doom to eclipse him,
the flaming swords of the sun scathing his weary
limbs, the sweat from his temples dripping in tiny

pools beside his eyes. At last he moved, he knelt up, and shielding his stricken eyes with one arm he gazed at the god, and saw now quite clearly a black butterfly resting on the lid of one of Sarkkon's eyes, inflecting its wings. He gave a grunt of comprehension and relief. He got up and went among the other figures. Close at hand they seemed fashioned of soft material, like camphor or wax, that was slowly dissolving, leaving them little more than stooks of clay, rough clod-like shapes of people, all but one figure which seemed fixed in coloured marble, a woman of beauty so wondrous to behold that the Assyrian bent his head in praise before her, though but an image of stone. When he looked again at it the black butterfly from the eyelid of the god fluttered between them and settled upon the girl's delicately carved lips for a moment, and then away. Amazedly watching it travel back to the idol he heard a movement and a sigh behind him. He leaped away, with his muscles distended, his fingers outstretched, and fear bursting in his eyes. The beautiful figure had moved a step towards him, holding out a caressing hand, calling him by name, his name!

'Talakku! Talakku!'

She stood thus almost as if again turned to stone

until his fear left him and he saw only her beauty, and knew only her living loveliness in a tunic of the sacred purple fringed with tinkling discs, that was clipped to her waist with a zone of gold and veiled, even in the stone, her secret hips and knees. The slender feet were guarded with pantoffles of crimson hide. Green agates in strings of silver hung beside her brows, depending from a fillet of gems that crowned and confined the black locks tightly curled. Buds of amber and coral were bound to her dusky wrists with threads of copper, and between the delicacy of her brown breasts an amulet of beryl, like a blue and gentle star, hung from a necklace made of balls of opal linked with amethysts.

'Wonder of god! who are you?' whispered the warrior; but while he was speaking she ran past him sweetly as an antelope to the dark god. He heard the clicking of her beads and gems as she bent in reverence kissing the huge stone feet of Sarkkon. He did not dare to approach her although her presence filled him with rapture; he watched her obeisant at the shrine and saw that one of her crimson shoes had slipped from the clinging heel. What was she—girl or goddess, phantom or spirit of the stone, or just some lunatic of the desert? But whatever she was it was marvellous, and the marvel of it shocked him; time seemed to seethe in every channel of his blood. He heard her again call out his name as if from very far away.

'Talakku!'

He hastened to lift her from the pavement, and conquering his tremors he grasped and lifted her roughly, as a victor might hale a captive.

'Pretty antelope, who are you?'

She turned her eyes slowly upon his—this was no captive, no phantom—his intrepid arms fell back weakly to his sides.

'You will not know me, O brave Assyrian captain,' said the girl gravely. 'I was a weaver in the city of Eridu . . .'

'Eridu!' It was an ancient city heard of only in the old poems of his country, as fabulous as snow in Canaan.

'Ai . . . it is long since riven into dust. I was a slave in Eridu, not . . . not a slave in spirit. . . .'

'Beauty so rare is nobility enough,' he said shyly.

'I worshipped god Namu-Sarkkon—behold his shrine. Who loves Namu-Sarkkon becomes what he wishes to become, gains what he wishes to gain.'

'I have heard of these things,' exclaimed the Assyrian. 'What did you gain, what did you wish to become?'

'I worshipped here desiring in my heart to be loved by the King of the World.'

'Who is he?'

She dropped her proud glances to the earth before him.

'Who was this King of the World?'

Still she made no reply nor lifted her eyes.

'Who are these figures that stand with us here?' he asked.

'Dead, all dead,' she sighed, 'their destinies have closed. Only I renew the destiny.'

She took his hand and led him among the wasting images.

'Merchants and poets, dead; princesses and slaves, dead; soldiers and kings, they look on us with eyes of dust, dead, all dead. I alone of Sarkkon's worshippers live on enduringly; I desired only love. I feed my spirit with new desire. I am the beam of his eye.'

'Come,' said the Assyrian suddenly, 'I will carry you to Shinar; set but my foot to that lost track . . . will you?'

She shook her head gravely. 'All roads lead to Sarkkon.'

'Why do we tarry here? Come.'

'Talakku, there is no way hence, no way for you,

no way for me. We have wandered into the boundless. What star returns from the sky, what drop from the deep?'

Talakku looked at her with wonder, until the longing in his heart lightened the shadow of his doom.

'Tell me what I must do,' he said.

She turned her eyes towards the dark god. 'He knows,' she cried, seizing his hands and drawing him towards the idol. 'Come, Talakku.'

'No, no!' he said in awe, 'I cannot worship there. Who can deny the gods of his home and escape vengeance? In Shinar, beloved land, goes not one bee unhived nor a bird without a bower. Shall I slip my allegiance at every gust of the desert?'

For a moment a look of anguish appeared in her eyes.

'But if you will not leave this place,' he continued gently, 'suffer me to stay.'

'Talakku, in a while I must sink again into the stone.'

'By all the gods I will keep you till I die,' he said. 'One day at least I will walk in Paradise.'

'Talakku, not a day, not an hour; moments, moments, there are but moments now.'

'Then, I am but dead,' he cried, 'for in that stone

[72]

your sleeping heart will never dream of me.'

'O, you whip me with rods of lilies. Quick, Talakku.' He knew in her urgent voice the divining hope with which she wooed him. Alas for the Assyrian, he was but a man whose dying lips are slaked with wise honey. He embraced her as in a dream under the knees of towering Sarkkon. Her kisses, wrapt in the delicate veils of love, not the harsh brief glister of passion, were more lulling than a thousand songs of lost Shinar, but the time's sweet swiftness pursued them. Her momentary life had flown like a rushing star, swift and delighting but doomed. From the heel of the god a beetle of green lustre began to creep towards them.

'Farewell, Talakku,' cried the girl. She stood again in her place before Namu-Sarkkon. 'Have no fear, Talakku, prince of my heart. I will lock up in your breast all my soft unsundering years. Like the bird of fire they will surely spring again.'

He waited, dumb, beside her, and suddenly her limbs compacted into stone once more. At the touch of his awed fingers her breast burned with the heat of the sun instead of the wooing blood. Then the vast silence of the world returned upon him; he looked in trembling loneliness at the stark sky, the unending desert, at the black god whose eye seemed to flicker balefully at him. Talakku turned to the lovely girl, but once more amazement gathered in all his veins. No longer stood her figure there—in its place he beheld only a stone image of himself.

'This is the hour, O beauteous one!' murmured the Assyrian, and, turning again towards the giant, he knelt in humility. His body wavered, faltered, suddenly stiffened, and then dissolved into a little heap of sand.

The same wind that unsealed Namu-Sarkkon and his shrine returning again at eve covered anew the idol and its figures, and the dust of the Assyrian captain became part of the desert for evermore.

. . . and in the whole of his days, vividly at the end of the afternoon—he repeated it again and again to himself—the kind country spaces had *never* absorbed *quite* so rich a glamour of light, so miraculous a bloom of clarity. He could feel streaming in his own mind, in his bones, the same crystalline brightness that lay upon the land. Thoughts and images went flowing through him as easily and amiably as fish swim in their pools; and as idly, too, for one of his speculations took up the theme of his family name. There was such an agreeable oddness about it, just as there was about all the luminous sky to-day, that it touched him as just a little remarkable. What *did* such a name connote, signify, or symbolize? It was a rann of a name, but it had euphony! Then again, like the fish, his ambulating fancy flashed into other shallows, and he giggled as he paused, peering at the buds in the brake. Turning back towards his house again he could see, beyond its roofs, the spire of the church tinctured richly as the vane: all round him was a new grandeur upon the grass of the

fields, and the spare trees had shadows below that
seemed to support them in the manner of a plinth,
more real than themselves, and the dykes and any
chance heave of the level fields were underlined, as
if for special emphasis, with long shades of mysterious blackness.

With a little drift of emotion that had at other
times assailed him in the wonder and ecstasy of pure
light, Jaffa Codling pushed through the slit in the
back hedge and stood within his own garden. The
gardener was at work. He could hear the voices of
the children about the lawn at the other side of the
house. He was very happy, and the place was beautiful, a fine white many-windowed house rising from
a lawn bowered with plots of mould, turreted with
shrubs, and overset with a vast walnut tree. This
house had deep clean eaves, a roof of faint coloured
slates that, after rain, glowed dully, like onyx or
jade, under the red chimneys, and half-way up at
one end was a balcony set with black balusters. He
went to a French window that stood open and
stepped into the dining-room. There was no one
within, and, on that lonely instant, a strange feeling
of emptiness dropped upon him. The clock ticked
almost as if it had been caught in some indecent act;
the air was dim and troubled after that glory

[76]

outside. Well, now, he would go up at once to his study and write down for his new book the ideas and images he had accumulated—beautiful rich thoughts they were—during that wonderful afternoon. He went to mount the stairs and he was passed by one of the maids; humming a silly song she brushed past him rudely, but he was an easy-going man—maids were unteachably tiresome—and reaching the landing he sauntered towards his room. The door stood slightly open and he could hear voices within. He put his hand upon the door . . . it would not open any further. What the devil . . . he pushed—like the bear in the tale—and he pushed, and he pushed—was there something against it on the other side? He put his shoulder to it . . . some wedge must be there, and *that* was extraordinary. Then his whole apprehension was swept up and whirled as by an avalanche—Mildred, his wife, was in there; he could hear her speaking to a man in fair soft tones and the rich phrases that could be used only by a woman yielding a deep affection to him. Codling kept still. Her words burned on his mind and thrilled him as if spoken to himself. There was a movement in the room, then utter silence. He again thrust savagely at the partly open door, but he could not

stir it. The silence within continued. He beat
upon the door with his fists, crying: 'Mildred,
Mildred!' There was no response, but he could
hear the rocking arm-chair commence to swing to
and fro. Pushing his hand round the edge of the
door he tried to thrust his head between the opening. There was not space for this, but he could just
peer into the corner of a mirror hung near, and
this is what he saw: the chair at one end of its
swing, a man sitting in it, and upon one arm of it
Mildred, the beloved woman, with her lips upon
the man's face, caressing him with her hands.
Codling made another effort to get into the room—
as vain as it was violent. 'Do you hear me, Mildred?' he shouted. Apparently neither of them
heard him; they rocked to and fro while he gazed
stupefied. What, in the name of God. . . . What
this . . . was she bewitched . . . were there such
things after all as magic, devilry!

He drew back and held himself quite steadily.
The chair stopped swaying and the room grew
awfully still. The sharp ticking of the clock in the
hall rose upon the house like the tongue of some
perfunctory mocker. Couldn't they hear the clock?
. . . Couldn't they hear his heart? He had to put
his hand upon his heart, for, surely, in that great

silence inside there, they would hear its beat, growing so loud now that it seemed almost to stun him!
Then in a queer way he found himself reflecting,
observing, analysing his own actions and intentions.
He found some of them to be just a little spurious,
counterfeit. He felt it would be easy, so perfectly
easy to flash in one blast of anger and annihilate the
two. He would do nothing of the kind. There
was no occasion for it. People didn't really do that
sort of thing, or, at least, not with a genuine
passion. There was no need for anger. His
curiosity was satisfied, quite satisfied, he was
certain; he had not the remotest interest in the
man. A welter of unexpected thoughts swept
upon his mind as he stood there. As a writer of
books he was often stimulated by the emotions and
impulses of other people, and now his own surprise
was beginning to intrigue him, leaving him, O,
quite unstirred emotionally, but interesting him
profoundly.

He heard the maid come stepping up the stairway
again, humming her silly song. He did not want
a scene, or to be caught eavesdropping, and so
turned quickly to another door. It was locked. He
sprang to one beyond it; the handle would not turn.
'Bah! what's *up* with 'em?' But the girl was now

upon him, carrying a tray of coffee things. 'O Mary!' he exclaimed casually, 'I . . .' To his astonishment the girl stepped past him as if she did not hear or see him, tapped upon the door of his study, entered, and closed the door behind her. Jaffa Codling then got really angry. 'Hell! were the blasted servants in it!' He dashed to the door again and tore at the handle. It would not even turn, and, though he wrenched with fury at it, the room was utterly sealed against him. He went away for a chair with which to smash the effrontery of that door. No, he wasn't angry, either with his wife or this fellow—Gilbert, she had called him— who had a strangely familiar aspect as far as he had been able to take it in; but when one's servants . . . faugh!

The door opened and Mary came forth smiling demurely. He was a few yards further along the corridor at that moment. 'Mary!' he shouted, 'leave the door open!' Mary carefully closed it and turned her back on him. He sprang after her with bad words bursting from him as she went towards the stairs and flitted lightly down, humming all the way as if in derision. He leaped downwards after her three steps at a time, but she trotted with amazing swiftness into the kitchen and slammed the door

in his face. Codling stood, but kept his hands carefully away from the door, kept them behind him.
'No, no,' he whispered cunningly, 'there's something fiendish about door handles to-day; I'll go
and get a bar, or a butt of timber,' and, jumping
out into the garden for some such thing, the miracle
happened to him. For it was nothing else than a
miracle, the unbelievable, the impossible, simple
and laughable if you will, but having as much
validity as any miracle can ever invoke. It was
simple and laughable because by all the known
physical laws he should have collided with his
gardener, who happened to pass the window with
his wheelbarrow as Codling jumped out on to the
path. And it was unbelievable that they should not,
and impossible that they *did* not collide; and it was
miraculous, because Codling stood for a brief
moment in the garden path and the wheelbarrow
of Bond, its contents, and Bond himself passed
apparently through the figure of Codling as if he
were so much air, as if he were not a living breathing man but just a common ghost. There was no
impact, just a momentary breathlessness. Codling
stood and looked at the retreating figure going on
utterly unaware of him. It is interesting to record
that Codling's first feelings were mirthful. He

[81]

giggled. He was jocular. He ran along in front of
the gardener, and let him pass through him once
more; then after him again; he scrambled into the
man's barrow, and was wheeled about by this incomprehensible thick-headed gardener who was
dead to all his master's efforts to engage his attention. Presently he dropped the wheelbarrow and
went away, leaving Codling to cogitate upon the
occurrence. There was no room for doubt, some
essential part of him had become detached from the
obviously not less vital part. He felt he was
essential because he was responding to the experience, he was reacting in the normal way to normal
stimuli, although he happened for the time being
to be invisible to his fellows and unable to communicate with them. How had it come about—
this queer thing? How could he discover what part
of him had cut loose, as it were? There was no
question of this being death, death wasn't funny,
it wasn't a joke; he had still all his human instincts.
You didn't get angry with a faithless wife or joke
with a fool of a gardener if you were dead, certainly not! He had realized enough of himself to
know he was the usual man of instincts, desires, and
prohibitions, complex and contradictory; his family
history for a million or two years would have

denoted that, not explicitly—obviously impossible
—but suggestively. He had found himself doing
things he had no desire to do, doing things he had
a desire *not* to do, thinking thoughts that had no
contiguous meanings, no meanings that could be
related to his general experience. At odd times he
had been chilled—aye, and even agreeably surprised
—at the immense potential evil in himself. But
still, this was no mere Jekyll and Hyde affair, that a
man and his own ghost should separately inhabit the
same world was a horse of quite another colour.
The other part of him was alive and active somewhere . . . as alive . . . as alive . . . yes, as *he*
was, but dashed if he knew where! What a lark
when they got back to each other and compared
notes! In his tales he had brooded over so many
imagined personalities, followed in the track of so
many psychological enigmas, that he *had* felt at times
a stranger to himself. What if, after all, that brood-
ing had given him the faculty of projecting this
figment of himself into the world of men? Or was
he some unrealized latent element of being without
its natural integument, doomed now to drift over
the ridge of the world for ever? Was it his per-
sonality, his spirit? Then how was the dashed thing
working? Here was he with the most wonderful

[83]

happening in human experience, and he couldn'
differentiate or disinter things. He was like a new
Adam flung into some old Eden.

There was Bond tinkering about with some plant
a dozen yards in front of him. Suddenly his three
children came round from the other side of the
house, the youngest boy leading them, carrying in
his hand a small sword which was made, not of
steel, but of some more brightly shining material
indeed it seemed at one moment to be of gold, and
then again of flame, transmuting everything in its
neighbourhood into the likeness of flame, the hair
of the little girl Eve, a part of Adam's tunic; and
the fingers of the boy Gabriel as he held the sword
were like pale tongues of fire. Gabriel, the youngest boy, went up to the gardener and gave the sword
into his hands, saying: 'Bond, is this sword any
good?' Codling saw the gardener take the weapon
and examine it with a careful sort of smile; his great
gnarled hands became immediately transparent, the
blood could be seen moving diligently about the
veins. Codling was so interested in the sight that
he did not gather in the gardener's reply. The little
boy was dissatisfied and repeated his question: 'No,
but, Bond, *is* this sword any good?' Codling rose,
and stood by, invisible. The three beautiful chil-

dren were grouped about the great angular figure of
the gardener in his soiled clothes, looking up now
into his face, and now at the sword, with anxiety
in all their puckered eyes. 'Well, Marse Gabriel,'
Codling could hear him reply, 'as far as a sword
goes, it may be a good un, or it may be a bad un,
but, good as it is, it can never be anything but a bad
thing.' He then gave it back to them; the boy
Adam held the haft of it, and the girl Eve rubbed
the blade with curious fingers. The younger boy
stood looking up at the gardener with unsatisfied
gaze. 'But, Bond, *can't* you say if this sword's any
good?' Bond turned to his spade and trowels.
'Mebbe the shape of it's wrong, Marse Gabriel,
though it seems a pretty handy size.' Saying this he
moved off across the lawn. Gabriel turned to his
brother and sister and took the sword from them;
they all followed after the gardener and once more
Gabriel made inquiry: 'Bond, is this sword any
good?' The gardener again took it and made a few
passes in the air like a valiant soldier at exercise.
Turning then, he lifted a bright curl from the head
of Eve and cut it off with a sweep of the weapon.
He held it up to look at it critically and then let it
fall to the ground. Codling sneaked behind him
and, picking it up, stood stupidly looking at it.

'Mebbe, Marse Gabriel,' the gardener was saying 'it ud be better made of steel, but it has a smartish edge on it.' He went to pick up the barrow, but Gabriel seized it with a spasm of anger, and cried out: 'No, no, Bond, will you say, just yes or no, Bond, is this sword any *good*?' The gardener stood still, and looked down at the little boy, who repeated his question—'just yes or no, Bond!' 'No, Marse Gabriel!' 'Thank you, Bond,' replied the child with dignity, 'that's all we wanted to know,' and, calling to his mates to follow him, he ran away to the other side of the house.

Codling stared again at the beautiful lock of hair in his hand, and felt himself grow so angry that he picked up a strange-looking flower-pot at his feet and hurled it at the retreating gardener. It struck Bond in the middle of the back and, passing clear through him, broke on the wheel of his barrow, but Bond seemed to be quite unaware of this catastrophe. Codling rushed after, and, taking the gardener by the throat, he yelled, 'Damn you, will you tell me what all this means?' But Bond proceeded calmly about his work unnoticing, carrying his master about as if he were a clinging vapour, or a scarf hung upon his neck. In a few moments, Codling dropped exhausted to the ground. 'What

. . . O Hell . . . what, what am I to do?' he groaned. 'What has happened to me? What shall I *do*? What *can* I do?' He looked at the broken flower-pot. 'Did I invent that?' He pulled out his watch. 'That's a real watch. I hear it ticking, and it's six o'clock.' Was he dead or disembodied or mad? What was this infernal lapse of identity? And who the devil, yes, who was it upstairs with Mildred? He jumped to his feet and hurried to the window; it was shut; to the door, it was fastened; he was powerless to open either. Well! well! this was experimental psychology with a vengeance, and he began to chuckle again. He'd have to write to McDougall about it. Then he turned and saw Bond wheeling across the lawn towards him again. '*Why* is that fellow always shoving that infernal green barrow around?' he asked, and, the fit of fury seizing him again, he rushed towards Bond, but, before he reached him, the three children danced into the garden again, crying, with great excitement, 'Bond, O, Bond!' The gardener stopped and set down the terrifying barrow; the children crowded about him, and Gabriel held out another shining thing, asking: 'Bond, is this box any good?' The gardener took the box and at once his eyes lit up with interest and delight. 'O, Marse

Gabriel, where'd ye get it?' 'Bond,' said the boy impatiently, 'is the box any *good*?' 'Any good?' echoed the man. 'Why, Marse Gabriel, Marse Adam, Miss Eve, look yere!' Holding it down in front of them, he lifted the lid from the box and a bright-coloured bird flashed out and flew round and round above their heads. 'O,' screamed Gabriel with delight, 'it's a kingfisher!' 'That's what it is,' said Bond, 'a kingfisher!' 'Where?' asked Adam. 'Where?' asked Eve. 'There it flies—round the fountain—see it? see it?' 'No,' said Adam. 'No,' said Eve.

'O, do, do, see it,' cried Gabriel; 'here it comes, it's coming!' and, holding his hands on high, and standing on his toes, the child cried out as happy as the bird which Codling saw flying above them.

'I can't see it,' said Adam.

'Where is it, Gaby?' asked Eve.

'O, you stupids,' cried the boy. '*There* it goes. There it goes . . . there . . . it's gone!'

He stood looking brightly at Bond, who replaced the lid.

'What shall we do now?' he exclaimed eagerly. For reply, the gardener gave the box into his hand, and walked off with the barrow. Gabriel took the box over to the fountain. Codling, unseen, went after him, almost as excited as the boy; Eve and her brother followed. They sat upon the stone tank that held the falling water. It was difficult for the child to unfasten the lid; Codling attempted to help him, but he was powerless. Gabriel looked up into his father's face and smiled. Then he stood up and said to the others:

'Now, *do* watch it this time.'

They all knelt carefully beside the water. He lifted the lid and, behold, a fish like a gold carp, but made wholly of fire, leaped from the box into the fountain. The man saw it dart down into the water, he saw the water bubble up behind it, he heard the hiss that the junction of fire and water produces, and saw a little track of steam follow the bubbles about the tank until the figure of the fish was consumed and disappeared. Gabriel, in ecstasies, turned to his sister with blazing happy eyes, exclaiming:

'There! Evey!'

'What was it?' asked Eve, nonchalantly. "I didn't see anything.'

'More didn't I,' said Adam.

'Didn't you see that lovely fish?'

'No,' said Adam.

'No,' said Eve.

'O, stupids,' cried Gabriel, 'it went right past the bottom of the water.'

'Let's get a fishin' nook,' said Adam.

'No, no, no,' said Gabriel, replacing the lid of the box. 'O no.'

Jaffa Codling had remained on his knees staring at the water so long that, when he looked around him again, the children had gone away. He got up and went to the door, and that was closed; the windows, fastened. He went moodily to a garden bench and sat on it with folded arms. Dusk had begun to fall into the shrubs and trees, the grass to grow dull, the air chill, the sky to muster its gloom. Bond had overturned his barrow, stalled his tools in the lodge, and gone to his home in the village. A curious cat came round the house and surveyed the man who sat chained to his seven-horned dilemma. It grew dark and fearfully silent. Was the world empty now? Some small thing, a snail perhaps, crept among the dead leaves in the hedge, with a sharp, irritating noise. A strange flood of mixed thoughts poured through his mind until at last one idea disentangled itself, and he began thinking with tremendous fixity of little Gabriel. He wondered if he could brood or meditate, or 'will' with sufficient power to bring him into the garden

again. The child had just vaguely recognized him
for a moment at the waterside. He'd try that dodge,
telepathy was a mild kind of a trick after so much of
the miraculous. If he'd lost his blessed body, at
least the part that ate and smoked and talked to
Mildred . . . He stopped as his mind stumbled on
a strange recognition. . . . What a joke, of course
. . . idiot . . . not to have seen *that*. He stood up
in the garden with joy . . . of course, *he* was upstairs with Mildred, it was himself, the other bit of
him, that Mildred had been talking to. What a
howling fool he'd been.

He found himself concentrating his mind on the
purpose of getting the child Gabriel into the garden
once more, but it was with a curious mood that
he endeavoured to establish this relationship. He
could not fix his will into any calm intensity of
power, or fixity of purpose, or pleasurable mental
ecstasy. The utmost force seemed to come with
a malicious threatening splenetic 'entreaty'. That
damned snail in the hedge broke the thread of his
meditation; a dog began to bark sturdily from a
distant farm; the faculties of his mind became joggled
up like a child's picture puzzle, and he brooded unin-
telligibly upon such things as skating and steam
engines, and Elizabethan drama so lapped about with

themes like jealousy and chastity. Really now, Shakespeare's Isabella was the most consummate snob in . . . He looked up quickly to his wife's room and saw Gabriel step from the window to the balcony as if he were fearful of being seen. The boy lifted up his hands and placed the bright box on the rail of the balcony. He looked up at the faint stars for a moment or two, and then carefully released the lid of the box. What came out of it and rose into the air appeared to Codling to be just a piece of floating light, but as it soared above the roof he saw it grow to be a little ancient ship, with its hull and fully-set sails and its three masts all of faint primrose flame colour. It cleaved through the air, rolling slightly as a ship through the wave, in widening circles above the house, making a curving ascent until it lost the shape of a vessel and became only a moving light hurrying to some sidereal shrine. Codling glanced at the boy on the balcony, but in that brief instant something had happened, the ship had burst like a rocket and released three coloured drops of fire which came falling slowly, leaving beautiful grey furrows of smoke in their track. Gabriel leaned over the rail with out-stretched palms, and, catching the green star and the blue one as they drifted down to him, he ran

with a rill of laughter back into the house. Codling
sprang forward just in time to catch the red star;
it lay vividly blasting his own palm for a monstrous
second, and then, slipping through, was gone. He
stared at the ground, at the balcony, the sky, and
then heard an exclamation . . . his wife stood at
his side.

'Gilbert! How you frightened me!' she cried.
'I thought you were in your room; come along
in to dinner.' She took his arm and they walked
up the steps into the dining-room together. 'Just
a moment,' said her husband, turning to the door
of the room. His hand was upon the handle, which
turned easily in his grasp, and he ran upstairs to his
own room. He opened the door. The light was on,
the fire was burning brightly, a smell of cigarette
smoke about, pen and paper upon his desk, the
Japanese book-knife, the gilt matchbox, everything
all right, no one there. He picked up a book from
his desk . . . *Monna Vanna*. His bookplate was in
it—*Ex Libris—Gilbert Cannister*. He put it down
beside the green dish; two yellow oranges were
in the green dish, and two most deliberately green
Canadian apples rested by their side. He went to
the door and swung it backwards and forwards quite
easily. He sat on his desk trying to piece the thing

together, glaring at the print and the book-knife and the smart matchbox, until his wife came up behind him exclaiming: 'Come along, Gilbert!'

'Where are the kids, old man?' he asked her.

Before she could reply he hurried along to the nursery. He saw the two cots, his boy in one, his girl in the other. He turned whimsically to Mildred, saying, 'There *are* only two, *are* there?' Such a question did not call for reply, but he confronted her as if expecting some assuring answer. She was staring at him with her bright beautiful eyes.

'Are there?' he repeated.

'How strange you should ask me that now!' she said. . . . 'If you're a very good man . . . perhaps . . .'

'Mildred!'

She nodded brightly.

He sat down in the rocking chair, but got up again saying to her gently—'We'll call him Gabriel.'

'But, suppose—'

'No, no,' he said, stopping her lovely lips, 'I know all about him.' And he told her a pleasant little tale.

PRINCESS OF KINGDOM GONE

LONG ago a princess ruled over a very tiny kingdom, too small, indeed, for ambition. Had it been larger she might have been a queen, and had it been seven times larger, so people said, she would certainly have been an empress. As it was, the barbarians referred to her country as 'that field!', or put other indignities upon it which, as she was high-minded, the princess did not heed, or, if she did heed, had too much pride to acknowledge.

In other realms her mansion, her beautiful mansion, would have been called a castle, or even a palace, so high was the wall, crowned with pink tiles, that enclosed and protected it from evil. The common gaze was warded from the door by a grove of thorns and trees, through which an avenue curved a long way round from the house to the big gate. The gate was of knotted oak, but it had been painted and grained most cleverly to represent some other fabulous wood. There was this inscription upon it: NO HAWKERS, NO CIRCULARS, NO GRATUITIES. Everybody knew the princess had not got any of these

things, but it was because they also knew the
mansion had no throne in it that people sneered,
really—but how unreasonable; you might just as
well grumble at a chime that hadn't got a clock!
As the princess herself remarked—'What *is* a throne
without high-mindedness!'—hinting, of course, at
certain people whom I dare not name. Behind the
mansion lay a wondrous garden, like the princess
herself above everything in beauty. A very private
bower was in the midst of it, guarded with corridors
of shaven yew and a half-circle hedge of arbutus and
holly. A slim river flowed, not by dispensation but
by accident, through the bower, and the bed and
bank of it, screened by cypresses, had been lined,
not by accident but by design—so strange are the
workings of destiny—with tiles and elegant steps
for a bathing pool. Here the princess, when the
blazon of the sun was enticing, used to take off her
robes of silk and her garments of linen and walk
about the turf of the bower around the squinancy
tree before slipping into the dark velvet water.

One day when she stepped out from the pool she
discovered a lot of crimson flower petals clinging
to her white skin. 'How beautiful they are,' she
cried, picking up her mirror, 'and where do they
come from?' As soon as convenient she inquired

upon this matter of her Lord Chancellor, a man
named Smith who had got on very well in life but
was a bit of a smudge.

'Crimson petals in the bath!'

'Yes, they have floated down with the stream.'

'How disgusting! Very! I'll make instant
inquiries!'

He searched and he searched—he was very
thorough was Smith—but though his researches
took no end of time, and he issued a bulky dossier
commanding all and sundry to attach the defiant
person of the miscreant or miscreants who had
defiled the princess's bath stream or pool with
refuse detritus or scum, offering, too, rewards for
information leading to his, her, or their detection,
conviction, and ultimate damnation, they availed
him not. The princess continued to bathe and to
emerge joyfully from the stream covered with
petals and looking as wonderful as a crimson
leopard. She caught some of the petals with a silver
net; she dried them upon the sunlight and hid them
in the lining of her bed, for they were full of
acrid but pleasing odours. So she herself early one
morning walked abroad, early indeed, and passed
along the river until she came to the field adjoining
the mansion. Very sweet and strange the world

seemed in the quiet after dawn. She stopped beside a half-used rick to look about her; there was a rush of surprised wings behind the stack and a thousand starlings fled up into the air. She heard their wings beating the air until they had crossed the river and dropped gradually into an elm tree like a black shower. Then she perceived a tall tree shining with crimson blooms and long dark boughs bending low upon the river. Near it a tiny red cottage stood in the field like a painted box, surrounded by green triangular bushes. It was a respectable looking cottage, named *River View*. On her approach the door suddenly opened, and a youth with a towel, just that and nothing more, emerged. He took flying rejoicing leaps towards the flaming tree, sprung upon its lowest limb and flung himself into the stream. He glided there like a rod of ivory, but a crimson shower fell from the quivering tree and veiled the pleasing boy until he climbed out upon the opposite bank and stood covered, like a leopard, with splendid crimson scars. The princess dared peer no longer; she retraced her steps, musing homewards to breakfast, and was rude to Smith because he was such a fool not to have discovered the young man who lived next door under the mysterious tree.

[98]

At the earliest opportunity she left a card at *River View*. Narcissus was the subject's name, and in due time he came to dinner, and they had green grapes and black figs, nuts like sweet wax and wine like melted amethysts. The princess loved him so much that he visited her very often and stayed very late. He was only a poet and she a princess, so she could not possibly marry him although this was what she very quickly longed to do; but as she was only a princess, and he a poet clinking his golden spurs, he did not want to be married to her. He had thick curling locks of hair red as copper, the mild eyes of a child, and a voice that could outsing a thousand delightful birds. When she heard his soft laughter in the dim delaying eve he grew strange and alluring to the princess. She knew it was because he was so beautiful that everybody loved him and wanted to win and keep him, but he had no inclination for anything but his art—which was to express himself. That was very sad for the princess; to be able to retain nothing of him but his poems, his fading images, while he himself eluded her as the wind eludes all detaining arms, forest and feather, briar and down of a bird. He did not seem to be a man at all but just a fairy image that slipped from her arms, gone, like brief music in the moonlight, before she was aware.

When he fell sick she watched by his bed.

'Tell me,' she murmured, her wooing palms caressing his flaming hair, 'tell me you love me.'

All he would answer was: 'I dream of loving you, and I love dreaming of you, but how can I tell if I love you?'

Very tremulous but arrogant she demanded of him: 'Shall I not know if you love me at all?'

'Ask the fox in your brake, the hart upon your mountain. I can never know if you love *me*.'

'I have given you my deepest vows, Narcissus; love like this is wider than the world.'

'The same wind blows in desert as in grove.'

'You do not love at all.'

'Words are vain, princess, but when I die, put these white hands like flowers about my heart; if I dream the unsleeping dream I will tell you there.'

'My beloved,' she said, 'if you die I will put upon your grave a shrine of silver, and in it an ark of gold jewelled with green garnets and pink sapphires. My spirit should dwell in it alone and wait for you; until you come back again I could not live.'

The poet died.

The princess was wild with grief, but she commanded her Lord Chancellor and he arranged magnificent obsequies. The shrine of silver and the ark of jewelled gold were ordered, a grave dug in a new planted garden more wonderful that the princess's bower, and a *To Let* bill appeared in the window of *River View*. At last Narcissus, with great pomp, was buried, the shrine and the ark of gold were clapped down upon him, and the princess in blackest robes was led away weeping on the arm of Smith—Smith was wonderful.

The sun that evening did not set—it mildly died out of the sky. Darkness came into the meadows, the fogs came out of them and hovered over the river and the familiar night sounds began. The princess sat in the mansion with a lonely heart from which all hopes were receding; no, not receding, she could see only the emptiness from which all her hopes had gone.

At midnight the spirit of Narcissus in its cerecloth rose up out of the grave, frail as a reed; rose out of its grave and stood in the cloudy moonlight beside the shrine and the glittering ark. He tapped upon the jewels with his fingers but there was no sound came from it, no fire, no voice. 'O holy love,' sighed the ghost, 'it is true what I feared, it is true, alas, it is true!' And lifting again his vague arm he crossed out the inscription on his tomb and wrote there instead with a grey and crumbling finger his last poem:

[101]

Pride and grief in your heart,
Love and grief in mine.

Then he crept away until he came to the bower
in the princess's garden. It was all silent and cold;
the moon was touching with brief beam the paps of
the plaster Diana. The ghost laid himself down to
rest for ever beneath the squinancy tree, to rest and
to wait; he wanted to forestall time's inscrutable
awards. He sank slowly into the earth as a knot
of foam slips through the beach of the seashore.
Deep down he rested and waited.

Day after day, month after month, the constant
princess went to her new grove of lamentation.
The grave garden was magnificent with holy flowers,
the shrine polished and glistening, the inscription
crisp and clear—the ghost's erasure being vain for
mortal eyes. In the ark she knew her spirit brooded
and yearned, she fancied she could see its tiny
flame behind the garnets and sapphires, and in a way
this gave her happiness. Meanwhile her own once
happy bower was left to neglect. The bolt rusted
in its gate, the shrubs rioted, tree trunks were
crusted with oozy fungus, their boughs cracked to
decay, the rose fell rotten, and toads and vermin
lurked in the desolation of the glades. 'Twas pitiful;
'twas as if the heart of the princess had left its

pleasant bower and had indeed gone to live in her costly shrine.

In the course of time she was forced to go away on business of state and travelled for many months; on her return the face of the Lord Chancellor was gloomy with misery. The golden ark had been stolen. Alarm and chagrin filled the princess. She went to the grave. It too had now grown weedy and looked forlorn. It was as if her own heart had been stolen away from her. 'Oh,' she moaned, 'what does it matter!' and, turning away, went home to her bower. There, among that sad sight, she saw a strange new tree almost in bloom. She gave orders for the pool to be cleansed and the bower restored to its former beauty. This was done, and on a bright day when the blazon of the sun was kind she went into the bower again, flung her black robes from her, and slipped like a rod of ivory into the velvet water. There were no blooms to gather now, though she searched with her silver net, but as she walked from the pool her long hair caught in the boughs of the strange tall squinancy tree, and in the disentangling it showered upon her beautiful crimson blooms that as they fell lingered upon her hips, her sweet shoulders, and kissed her shining knees.

COMMUNION

He was of years calendared in unreflecting minds as tender years, and he was clothed in tough corduroy knickerbockers, once the habiliments of a huger being, reaching to the tops of some boots shod with tremendous nails and fastened by bits of fugitive string. His jacket was certainly the jacket of a child —possibly some dead one, for it was not his own— and in lieu of a collar behold a twist of uncoloured, unclean flannel. Pink face, pink hands, yellow hair, a quite unredeemable dampness about his small nose—altogether he was a country boy.

'What are you doing there, Tom Prowse?' asked Grainger, the sexton, entering to him suddenly one Saturday afternoon. The boy was sitting on a bench in the empty nave, hands on knees, looking towards the altar. He rose to his feet and went timidly through the doorway under the stern glance of that tall tall man, whose height enabled him to look around out of a grave when it was completely dug. 'You pop on out of 'ere,' said Grainger, threateningly, but to himself, when the boy had gone.

[104]

Walking into the vestry Grainger emptied his pockets of a number of small discarded bottles and pots of various shapes and uses—ink-bottles, bottles for gum and meat extract, fish-paste pots, and tins which had contained candy. He left them there. The boy, after he had watched him go away, came back and resumed his seat behind one of the round piers.

A lady dressed in black entered and, walking to the front stall under the pulpit, knelt down. The boy stared at the motionless figure for a long time until his eyes ached and the intense silence made him cough a little. He was surprised at the booming hollow echo and coughed again. The lady continued bowed in her place; he could hear her lips whispering sibilantly: the wind came into the porch with sudden gust and lifted the arras at the door. Turning he knocked his clumsy boots against the bench. After that the intense silence came back again, humming in his ears and almost stopping his breath, until he heard footsteps on the gravel path. The vicar's maid entered and went towards the vestry. She wished to walk softly when she observed the kneeling lady, but her left shoe squeaked stubbornly as she moved, and both heels and soles echoed in sharp tones along the tiles of the chancel. The boy heard the rattle of a bucket handle and saw the maid place the bucket beside the altar and fetch flowers and bottles and pots from the vestry. Some she stood upon the table of the altar; others, tied by pieces of string, she hung in unique positions upon the front and sides, filling them with water from the pail as she did so; and because the string was white, and the altar was white, and the ugly bottles were hidden in nooks of moss, it looked as if the very cloth of the altar sprouted with casual bloom.

Not until the maid had departed did the lady who had been bowed so long lift up her head adoringly towards the brass cross; the boy overheard her deep sigh; then she, too, went away, and in a few moments more the boy followed and walked clumsily, thoughtfully, to his home.

His father was the village cobbler. He was a widower, and he was a freethinker, too; no mere passive rejector of creeds, but an active opponent with a creed of his own, which if less violent was not less bigoted than those he so witheringly decried. The child Tom had never been allowed to attend church; until to-day, thus furtively, he had never even entered one, and in the day school religious instruction had been forbidden by his

[106]

atheistic father. But while faith goes on working its miracles the whirligigs of unfaith bring on revenges. The boy now began to pay many secret visits to the church. He would walk under the western tower and slip his enclosing palms up and down the woolly rope handles, listen to the slow beat of the clock, and rub with his wristband the mouldings of the brass lectern with the ugly bird on a ball and the three singular chubby animals at the foot, half ox, half dog, displaying monstrous teeth. He scrutinized the florid Georgian memorial fixed up the wall, recording the virtues, which he could not read, of a departed Rodney Giles; made of marble, there were two naked fat little boys with wings; they pointed each with one hand towards the name, and with the other held a handkerchief each to one tearful eye. This was very agreeable to young Prowse, but most he loved to sit beside one of the pillars—the stone posties, he called them—and look at the window above the altar where for ever half a dozen angels postured rhythmically upon the ladder of Jacob.

One midsummer evening, after evensong, he entered for his usual meditation. He had no liking for any service or ritual; he had no apprehension of the spiritual symbols embodied in the building; he only liked to sit there in the quiet, gazing at things

[107]

in a dumb sort of way, taking, as it were, a bath of holiness. He sat a long time; indeed, so still was he, he might have been dozing as the legions of dead parishioners had dozed during interminable dead sermons. When he went to the door—the light having grown dim—he found it was locked. He was not at all alarmed at his situation: he went and sat down again. In ten minutes or so he again approached the door . . . it was still locked. Then he walked up the aisle to the chancel steps and crossed the choir for the first time. Choristers' robes were in the vestry, and soon, arrayed in cassock and surplice, he was walking with a singular little dignity to his old seat by one of the pillars. He sat there with folded hands, the church growing gloomier now; he climbed into the pulpit and turned over the leaves of the holy book; he sat in the choir-stalls, pretended to play the organ, and at last went before the altar and, kneeling at the rails, clasped his orthodox hands and murmured, as he had heard others murmuring there, a rigmarole of his scholastic hours:

Thirty days hath September,
April, June and November.
All the rest have thirty-one,
Excepting February alone,

And leap year coming once in four,
February then has one day more.

Re-entering the vestry, he observed on a shelf in
a niche a small loaf wrapped in a piece of linen. He
felt hungry and commenced to devour the bread,
and from a goblet there he drank a little sip of
sweet-tasting wine. He liked the wine very much,
and drank more and more of it.

There was nothing else to be done now in the
darkness, so he went on to the soft carpet within
the altar rails, and, piling up a few of the praying
mats from the choir—little red cushions they were,
stamped with black fleur-de-lys, which he admired
much in the daylight—he fell asleep.

And he slept long and deeply until out of some
wonderful place he began to hear the word 'Ruffian,
Ruffian,' shouted with anger and harshness. He was
pulled roughly to his feet, and apprehension was
shaken into his abominable little head.

The morning sunlight was coming through the
altar window, and the vicar's appearance was many-
coloured as a wheelwright's door; he had a green
face, and his surplice was scaled with pink and
purple gouts like a rash from some dreadful rain-
bow. And dreadful indeed was the vicar as he thrust
the boy down the altar steps into the vestry, hissing

as he did, 'Take off those things!' and darting back to throw the cushions into proper places to support the knees of the expected devotees.

'Now, how did you get in here?' he demanded, angrily.

The boy hung up the cassock: 'Some one locked me in last night, Sir.'

'Who was it?'

'I dunno, Sir; they locked me in all night.'

His interrogator glared at him for a moment in silence, and the boy could not forbear a yawn. Thereat the vicar seized him by the ear and, pulling it with such animation as to contort his own features as well as the child's, dragged him to the vestry door, gurgling with uncontrolled vexation, 'Get out of this. Get out . . . you . . . you beast!'

As the boy went blinking down the nave the tenor bell began to ring; the stone posties looked serene and imperturbable in new clean sunlight, and that old blackbird was chirping sweetly in the lilac at the porch.

THE QUIET WOMAN

IT was the loneliest place in the world, Hardross said. A little cogitation and much experience had given him the fancy that the ark of the kingdom of solitude was lodged in a lift, any lift, carrying a charter of mute passengers from the pavement to any sort of Parnassus. Nothing ever disturbs its velveteen progression; no one ever speaks to the lift man (unless it happens to be a lift girl). At Hardross's place of abode it happened to be a lift boy, sharp and white-faced, whose tough hair was swept backwards in a stiff lock from his brow, while his pert nose seemed inclined to pursue it. His name was Brown. His absences from duty were often coincident with the arrivals and departures of Mr. Hardross. His hands were brown enough if the beholder carried some charity in his bosom, but the aspect of his collar or his shoes engendered a deal of vulgar suspicion, and his conduct was at once inscrutable and unscrupulous. It may have been for this reason that Hardross had lately begun walking the whole downward journey from his high chamber, but it must have been something less capricious that caused him always to essay the corresponding upward flight. A fancy for exercise perhaps, for he was a robust musician, unmarried, and of course, at thirty-three or thirty-four, had come to the years of those indiscretions which he could with impunity and without reprobation indulge.

On the second floor, outside the principal door of one set of chambers, there always stood a small console table; it was just off the landing, in an alcove that covered two other doors, a little dark angular-limbed piece of furniture bearing a green lacquer dish of void visiting cards, a heap that seemed neither to increase nor dwindle but lay there as if soliciting, so naïvely, some further contributions. Two maiden ladies, the Misses Pilcher, who kept these rooms, had gone to France for a summer holiday, but though the flat had for the time being some new occupants the console table still kept its place, the dish of cards of course languishing rather unhopefully. The new tenants were also two ladies, but they were clearly not sisters and just as clearly not Pilcherly old maids. One of them, Hardross declared, was the loveliest creature he had ever seen. She was dark, almost tall, about as tall as

Hardross though a little less robust and rather more
graceful. Her mature scarlet lips and charming
mature eyes seemed always to be wanting to speak
to him. But she did not speak to him, ever, when
he modestly tried to overcome, well, not her
reserve—no one with such sparkling eyes could
possibly be reserved—but her silence. He often
passed her on the landing, but he did not hear her
voice, or music, or speech, or any kind of intercourse within the room. He called her The Quiet
Woman. The other lady, much older, was seldom
seen; she was of great dignity. The younger one
walked like a woman conscious and proud of the
beauty underneath her beautiful clothes; the soft
slippers she wore seemed charged with that silent
atmosphere. Even the charwoman who visited
them daily and rattled and swept about was sealed
of the conspiracy of silence; at least he never caught
—though it must be confessed that he guiltily tried
—the passage of a single word. What was the
mystery of the obstinately silent ménage? Did the
elder lady suffer from sorrow or nerves; was she
under a vow; was she a genius writing a sublime
book?

The voiceless character of the intercourse did not
prevent Hardross becoming deeply enamoured and

at the same time deeply baffled. Morning and evening as he went to the great city church of which he was organist he would often catch a glimpse of his quiet woman on the stairs. At favourable junctures he had lifted his hat and said Good-morning or Good-evening, but she had turned away as if overcome by confusion or an excess of propriety.

'I am a coward,' he would think; 'shyness and diffidence rule me, they curse me, they ruin my life; but she, good heavens! is extraordinarily retiring. Why, I am just a satyr, a rampant raging satyr, a satyr!' And he would liken her to Diana, always darting with such fawnlike modesty from the alcove whenever he approached. He did not even know her name. He wanted to inquire of the lift boy Brown or the porter, but there again he lacked the casual touch to bring off the information. The boy was too young, too cute, too vulgar, and the porter too taciturn, as difficult for Hardross to approach as an archbishop would have been. But Miss Barker now, that milliner, down below on the ground floor! She would know; she knew everybody and everything about the chambers, including, quite familiarly, Hardross himself—she would be sure to know. But even she would have to be approached with discrimination.

'Evening, Miss Barker!' he cried. The good-looking spinster peered up from a half-trimmed bonnet. 'When do *you* go for a holiday, then?'

'Holidays,' she sighed, though the corner of her mouth was packed with pins, 'I cannot afford holidays.'

'Ho, ho, you can't afford!'

Their common fund of repartee lay in his confident assumption that she was rolling in surplus income and her counter-assertion that she was stricken in poverty; that people—the pigs—would not pay her prices, or that those who did not flinch at her prices would not pay her bills.

'Astonishing, deplorable, this Mammon-worship!' he declared, leaning genially upon her table; 'you know, it breaks my heart to see you a slave to it, a woman of a thousand, ten thousand in fact. Give it up, O,'—he beat the table with his hand—'give it up before it is too late!'

'Too late for what?' she asked.

'Why, all the delightful things a woman like you could do.'

'As what?'

'O . . . travel, glories of nature, you know, friendship, men . . . love itself.'

'Give me all the money I want'—she was brusque

[115]

about it, and began to dab the unwanted pins back into their cushion—'and I'll buy, yes *buy*, a sweetheart for each day in the week.'

'Heavens now!' He was chilled by this implication of an experience that may have been dull, that must have been bitter, but he floundered on: 'What now would you give for me?'

'For you!' She contemplated him with gravity: 'To be sure I had not thought of you, not in that way.'

'O, but please *do* think of me, dear lady; put me in your deepest regard.'

The ghost of a knowing grin brushed her features. Really a charming woman, in parts. A little stout, perhaps, and she had fat red hands, but her heart was a good substantial organ, it was in the right place, and her features seemed the best for wear.

'You are one of those surprising ladies'—he plunged gaily—'who've a long stocking somewhere, with trunks full of shares and scrip, stocks at the bank and mortgages at your solicitor's. O yes, yes,' he cried out against her protestation, 'and you will make a strange will leaving it all to me!'

She shook her head hopelessly, bending again over the bonnet whose desperate skeleton she had clothed with a flounce of crimson velvet. She was very quiet.

'Have I been rude?' he hazarded. 'Forgive me.'

'Well, it's not true,' she insisted.

'Forgive me—I have hurt you—of course it's not true.'

Apparently she forgave him; he was soon asking if there were any rooms to let in the building. 'Furnished, I mean.' He gave rein to his naïve strategy: 'I have friends who want to come here and stay with me for a short holiday. I thought you might know of some.'

'In these flats?' She shook her head, but he persisted and played his artful card:

'The Miss Pilchers, on the second floor, haven't they gone away?'

She did not know—why not ask the porter.

'Yes, I must ask the porter, but I can never catch the porter, he is so fugitive, he is always cutting his lucky. I hate that man, don't you?'

And there, temporarily, he had to leave it.

So many days passed now without a glimpse of his lovely one that he had almost brought himself to the point of tapping at the door and inquiring after her welfare, only the mysterious air of the apartment—how strange, how soundless it was— forbade any such crudeness. One morning he recklessly took a cigarette from his case and laid it upon the console table as he passed. When he returned later the cigarette was gone; it had been replaced by a chocolate cream, just one, a big one. He snatched it away and rapturously ate it. Later in the day he was blessed by a deep friendly gaze, as she flitted into her room. Hardross rejoiced; in the morning he left another cigarette and was again rewarded.

'But, O God help me,' he thought, 'I can't go on like this!'

So he bought a whole box of bonbons, but his courage deserted him as he approached their door; he left the package upon the console table and slunk guiltily away. The next morning he observed a whole box of cigarettes, a well-known exquisite brand, laid temptingly there. He stretched his eager hand towards it, but paused. Could that be a gift for him? Heavens above! What were the miraculous gods about to shower upon him? Was this their delicate symbol? He could not believe it, no, he could not, he left the box lying there. And it lay there for hours, indeed, until he crept down and seized it. Afterwards he walked trembling into the brighter air and went for a long ride on the top of an omnibus. There had been no letter, but he fancied that he had got hold of a clue. 'Be very careful, Hardross my boy, this is too splendid to spoil.'

An afternoon or so later he met her coming into the hall, a delicious figure with gay parasol and wide white hat. He delayed her:

'Let me thank you, may I, for those perfect cigarettes?'

The lovely creature did not reply. She just smiled her recognition of him; she did not speak nor move away, she stood there quite silent and timid.

'I wonder,' he began again, 'if I might'—it sounded dreadfully silly to him, but having begun he went on—'if I might invite you to my church this evening, a rather special choral service, very jolly, you know. I'm the organist; would you come?'

No answer.

'Would you care to come?'

She lifted both her hands and touching her lips and ears with significant gestures shook her head ever so hopelessly at him.

'Deaf and dumb!' he exclaimed. Perhaps the shock of the revelation showed too painfully in his face, for she turned now sadly away. But the hall was divinely empty. He caught one of the exquisite hands and pressed it to his lips.

Thereafter Hardross walked about as if he too

were deaf and dumb, except for a vast effusion of sighs. He could praise that delicacy of the rarest whereby she had forborne to lure him, as she could so easily have done, into a relation so shrouded and so vague. But that did not solve his problem, it only solidified it. He wanted and awaited the inspiration of a gesture she could admire, something that would propitiate her delicacy and alarms. He did not want to destroy by clumsy persistencies the frail net of her regard for him; he was quite clear about that, the visible fineness of her quality so quelled him. Applying himself to the task, he took lessons in the alphabet language, that inductile response of fingers and thumbs.

Meanwhile she had marked her sense of the complication by hiding like a hurt bird, and although the mystery of the quiet rooms was now exposed she herself remained unseen. He composed a graceful note and left it upon the console table. The note disappeared but no reply came: she made no sign and he regretted his ardour.

Such a deadlock of course could not exist for ever, and one evening he met her walking up the stairs. She stopped mutually with him. He was carrying his music. He made a vain attempt to communicate with her by means of his finger alphabet, but she did not understand him although she delightedly made a reply on her fingers, which he was too recently initiated to interpret. They were again at a standstill: he could think of nothing to do except to open his book of organ music and show her the title-page. She looked it over very intelligently as he tried by signs to convey his desire to her, but he was certain she was blank about it all. He searched his pocket for a pencil—and swore at his non-success. There he stood like a fool, staring at her smiling face until to his amazement she took his arm and they descended the stairs; they were in the street together. He walked to the church on something vastly less substantial than air, and vastly superior.

Hardross's church was square and ugly, with large round-headed windows. Its entrance was up some steps between four Corinthian pillars upon the bases of which cabmen snoozed when it was warm, or coughed and puffed in the winter cold. There was a pump on the kerb and a stand for hackney cabs. A jungle of evergreens squatted in a railed corner under the tower, with a file of iris plants that never flowered. Upon the plinth of the columns a ribald boy had chalked:

REMOVE THIS OBSTACLE

Eternally at the porch tired cab-horses drooped and meditated, while the drivers cut hunches of bread and meat or cheese or onion and swallowed from their tin bottles the cold tea or other aliment associated with tin bottles. There was always a smell of dung at the entrance, and an aroma of shag tobacco from the cabmen's pipes curled into the nave whenever the door opened for worshippers. Inside the church Hardross ushered his friend to a seat that he could watch from his organ loft. There were few people present. He borrowed a lead pencil from a choirboy, and while the lesson was being perfunctorily intoned, sounding like some great voice baffled by its infinitely little mind, he scribbled on a sheet of paper the questions he was so eager to ask; what was her name and things like that:

How can we communicate? May I write to you? Will you to me? Excuse the catechism and scribble, but I want so much to know you and grab at this opportunity.

Yours devotedly

JOHN HARDROSS.

When he looked up her place was empty; she had gone away in the middle of the service. He hurried home at last very perturbed and much abashed, for it was not so much the perplexities of intercourse, the torment of his dilemma, that possessed him now as a sense of felicities forbidden and amenities declined.

But his fickle intelligence received a sharp admonitory nudge on the following evening when he espied her sitting in the same place at church for all the world as if she had not deserted it on the evening before. Then he remembered that of course she couldn't hear a thing—idiot he was to have invited her. Again she left the church before the close of the service. This for several days, the tantalized lover beholding her figure always hurrying from his grasp.

He pursued the practice of the deaf and dumb alphabet with such assiduity that he became almost apt in its use; the amount of affection and devotion that he could transcribe on finger and thumb was prodigious, he yearned to put it to the test. When at last he met her again in the hall he at once began spelling out things, absurd things, like: 'May I beg the honour of your acquaintance?' She watched this with interest, with excitement even, but a shadow of doubt crept into her lovely eyes. She moved her own fingers before him, but in vain; he could not interpret a single word, not one. He

was a dense fool; O how dense, how dense! he
groaned. But then he searched his pockets and
brought out the note he had scribbled in church. It
was a little the worse for wear, but he smoothed it,
and standing close by her side held it for her perusal.
Again his hopes were dashed. She shook her head,
not at all conclusively, but in a vague uncomprehending way. She even with a smile indicated her
need of a pencil, which he promptly supplied. To
his amazement what she scribbled upon the page
were some meaningless hieroglyphs, not letters,
though they were grouped as in words, but some
strange abracadabra. He looked so dismally at her
that she smiled again, folding the paper carefully ere
she passed on up the stairs.

Hardross was now more confounded than ever.
A fearful suspicion seized him: was she an idiot, was
it a mild insanity, were those marks just the nota-
tion of a poor diseased mind? He wished he had
kept that letter. God, what a tragedy! But as he
walked into the town his doubts about her intellect
were dispelled. Poof! only an imbecile himself
could doubt that beautiful staring intelligence. That
was not it; it was some jugglery, something to do
with those rooms. Nothing was solved yet, nothing
at all; how uncanny it was becoming!

He returned in the afternoon full of determination. Behold, like a favourable augury, the door by the console table stood open, wide open. It did occur to him that an open door might be a trap for unwary men, but he rapped the brass knocker courageously. Of course there was no response—how could there be—and he stepped inside the room. His glance had but just time to take in the small black piano, the dark carpet, the waxed margins of the floor, the floral dinginess of the walls brightened by mirrors and softened by gilt and crimson furniture, when the quiet woman, his Diana, came to him joyfully holding out both her hands. Well, there was no mystery here after all, nothing at all, although the elder lady was out and they were apparently alone. Hardross held her hands for some moments, the intensity of which was as deeply projected in her own eyes as in the tightness of his clasp. And there was tea for him! She was at her brightest, in a frock of figured muslin, and sitting before her he marvelled at the quickness of her understanding, the vividness of her gestures, the gentleness with which she touched his sleeve. That criminal suspicion of her sanity crowned him with infamy. Such communication was deliciously intimate; there came a moment when Hardross in a wild impulsive ecstasy flung himself before her, bowing his head in her lap. The quiet woman was giving him back his embraces, her own ardour was drooping beautifully upon him, when he heard a strange voice exclaim in the room: 'God is my help! Well then!' A rattle of strange words followed which he could not comprehend. He turned to confront the elder woman, who surveyed them with grim amusement. The other stood up, smiling, and the two women spoke in finger language. The new-comer began to remove her gloves, saying:

'It is Mr. Hardross, then. I am glad to meet. There is a lot of things to be spoken, eh?'

She was not at all the invalid he had half expected to find. She removed her hat and came back a competent-looking woman of about fifty, who had really an overwhelming stream of conversation. She took tea and, ignoring the girl as if she were a block of uncomprehending ornament, addressed herself to the interloper.

'You do not know me, Mr. Hardross?'

'It is a pleasure I have but looked forward to,' he replied, in the formal manner that at times irresistibly seized him, 'with the keenest possible anticipation and . . .'

'No, I am Madame Peshkov. We are from Odessa, do you know it? We go back to our Russia to-morrow; yes, it is true.'

His organs of comprehension began to crackle in his skull, but he went on stirring his fresh cup of tea and continued to do so for quite a long time.

'No, you . . . are . . . Russian! I did not know!' Amid his musing astonishment that fact alone was portentous; it explained so much, everything in fact, but how he could ever contrive to learn such a language was the question that agitated him, so fearfully difficult a language, and on his fingers too! Then that other thunderclap began to reverberate: they were going, when was it? To-morrow! All this while Madame Peshkov ran on with extravagant volubility. She had the habit of picking one of the hairpins from her hair and gently rubbing her scalp with the rounded end of it; she would replace the pin with a stylish tap of her fingers. It was a long time before Hardross extracted the pith from her remarks, and then only when the hypnotism induced by the stirring of his tea suddenly lapsed; he became aware of the dumb girl's gaze fixed piercingly upon him, while his own was drawn away by the force of the other's revelations. What he had already taken in was sad and strange. Her name was Julia Krasinsky. She was not at all related to Madame Peshkov, she was an orphan. Madame's own daughter had been deaf and dumb, too, and the girls has been inseparable companions until two years ago, when Natalia Peshkov had died—O, an unspeakable grief still. He gathered that Madame was a widow, and that since Natalia's death the two women had lived and travelled together. Madame talked on; it was tremendously exciting to Hardross crouching in his chair, but all that echoed in his mind were the words Julia Krasinsky, Julia Krasinsky, until she suddenly asked him:

'Do you love her?'

He was startled by this appalling directness; he stammered a little, but he finally brought out:

'I adore her. Beyond everything I deeply, deeply love her.' He then added: 'I feel shameful enough now. I rage inwardly. All these many weeks I have dallied like a boy. I did not understand the situation. I have wasted our chances, our time, and now you are going.'

'You can't waste time,' retorted the abrupt lady. 'Time deals with you no matter how you use his hours.'

'I suppose so,' he agreed quite helplessly, 'but we might have been extraordinary friends.'

'O, but you are, eh! She is bewitched, you cannot speak to her, she cannot speak to you, but yet you love. O, she is vairy vairy fond of you, Mr. Hardross. Why not? She has the best opinions of you.'

'Ah, she will change her opinion now. A fool like me?'

'No one ever changes an opinion. Your opinions govern and guide and change you. If they don't they are not worth holding. And most of them are not, eh, do you see, we are such fools, but God is our help.'

She talked confidently, intimately and quickly, but Hardross wished she would not do so, or use her hairpins in that absurd distracting way. He himself had no confidence; he was reserved by nature, irrevocably, and the mask of deliberation was necessary to him.

'Madame Peshkov, I shall take her out for a walk in the town, now, at once!' he cried.

'Ah, so?' Madame nodded her head vigorously, even approvingly. He had sprung up and approached the quiet woman. All her gentle nearness overcame him and he took her audaciously into his arms.

Not less eagerly she slid to his breast and clung there like a bird to the shelter of its tree. Julia turned to Madame Peshkov with a smiling apologetic shrug, as much as to say: 'What can one do with such a fellow, so strong he is, you see!' Madame bade him bring Julia later on to the café where they always dined.

His happiness was profound. He had never had an experience so moving as the adorable dumb woman by his side: yet so unsurprising, as if its possibility had always lain goldenly in his mind like an undreamed dream, or like music, half-remembered music. There was nothing, of course, just nothing they could talk about. They could look into shop windows together rather intimately, and they were a long time in a shady arcade of the park, full of lime-browsing bees, where they sat watching a peacock picking the gnats off the shrubs. It was the pleasantest possible defeat of time. Then there was the handsome girl crossing the yard of a weaving mill as they passed. She was carrying a great bale of bright blue wool and had glanced at them with a friendly smile. Her bare white arms encircled the wool: she had big gilt rings in her ears, and her fine shining chestnut-coloured hair was disarrayed and tumbled upon the bale. Julia

[130]

had pressed his arm with joy. Yes, she delighted
in the things he delighted in; and she felt too that
sense of sorrow that hung in the air about them.

Her appearance in the café stirred everybody like
a wave of sweet air. Hardross was filled with pride.
He felt that it was just so that she would enrich the
world wherever she wandered, that things would
respond to her appearance in astonishing mysterious
ways. Why, even the empty wine-glasses seemed
to behave like large flowers made miraculously out
of water, a marvel of crystal petals blooming but
for her; certainly the glasses on other tables didn't
look at all like these. He drank four glasses of wine
and after dinner they all sat together in the flat until
the half-darkness was come. And now Madame
Peshkov too was very silent; she sat smoking or
scratching her head with her pins. It was nine
o'clock, but there remained a preposterous glare in
the west that threw lateral beams against the tops of
tall buildings, although the pavements were already
dim. It made the fronts of the plastered houses over
the way look like cream cheese. Six scarlet
chimney-pots stood stolidly at attention—the torsos
of six guardsmen from whom head and limbs had
been unkindly smitten; the roof seemed to be rushing away from them. Beyond was an echo of the

sunset, faint in the northern sky. How sweet, how sad, to sit so silently in this tremulous gloom. It was only at the last when they parted at her door that the shadow of their division became omnipresent. Then it overwhelmed them.

Hardross crept upstairs to his own rooms. In such plights the mind, careless of time present and time past, full of an anguish that quenches and refills like a sponge, writhes beyond hope with those strange lesions of demeanour that confound the chronicler. Tra-la-la, sang the distracted man, snapping his sweating fingers in time with a ribald leering ditty, Tra-la-la. He dropped plumb to Atlantean depths of grief, only to emerge like a spouting whale with the maddening Tra-la-la tugging him, a hook in his body, from despair to dementia. He was roused from this vertiginous exercise by a knocking at his door. The door was thrust open, and Madame Peshkov asked if he was there. He rose up and switched on a light.

'What is to be done now?' cried the lady. If her silence below had been complete, as complete as poor Julia's, she was now fully audible and not a little agitated. 'What is to be done? I cannot believe it of her, but it is true, as true as God!'

Hardross beheld her sink, stricken with some

trouble, into an arm-chair, beating her hands together.

'I have no influence, gone it is, no power over her, none whatever. What is to be done? Assist us, please. She has been so . . . O, for days, and now it comes, it comes . . .'

'What has come?' he interrupted sharply.

'I cannot believe it of her, but it is true . . . as God. She is like a vast . . . cold . . . stone, a mountain.'

'Is this about Julia?'

'She will not go. Of course she will not go! She declines, she will not come back to Odessa. She says she will not come. I have to tell you this, Mr. Hardross, I cannot move her. She is like a vast . . . cold . . . stone. What, then?'

Madame's appeal seemed pregnant with a significance that he but dimly savoured. He asked: 'What is she going to do, then?'

'To stop in this England, here, in this very place! But our passages are booked, to-morrow it is—pooh, it does not matter!—I am to leave her here in this place, here she will stay, in a foreign land, without speech or understanding. But what is to be done, I ask of you?'

He was delirious himself; he kept whispering

Julia, Julia, but he managed to ask with a lugubrious covering of propriety:

'What? I don't know. Shall I go to her?'

'But can you not see? Do you comprehend, you, Hardross? O, it is a madness. I want to explain it to you, but it is all so gross, so swift, like a vulture. You see it is impossible for me to remain an hour longer, an hour in England, impossible absolutely; there are reasons, lives, perhaps, depending on my return. Yes, it is true; we live in Russia, do you see, and in Russia . . . ah, you understand! But how shall I leave this woman here?'

Madame stared at him with curious inquisitiveness, beating her hands upon the arm of the chair as if she expected an answer, a prompt one:

'Of course she will not go away from you now, of course, of course, she has never had a lover before —how could she, poor thing? I understand it, she is not a child. And you, Mr. Hardross, you are a generous man, you have courage; a good man, a man of his honour. O yes, it is true, I see it, I feel it, and so she will not be torn away from you now. I understand that, she is no longer a child.'

Madame rose and took him by the arm. 'Marry her, my friend! Do not you see? I can leave her to you. Marry her at once, marry her!' She stood

as if it were something that could be done on the
spot, as easy as giving one a cup of tea. But he did
not hesitate.

'Why, I would give my soul to do it!' he cried,
and rushed away down the stairs to Julia.

And surely she was as wise as she was beautiful,
and as rich as she was wise.

THE TRUMPETERS

THEY were crossing the Irish Sea. It was night, blowing a moderate gale, but the moon, aloft on the port bow with a wind, was chock-full of such astounding brightness that the turmoil of the dark waves was easy and beautiful to see. The boat was crowded with soldiers on leave; the few civilian passengers—mechanics, labourers, and a miner going to his home in Wexford, who had got drunk at the harbour inn before coming aboard—were congregated in the angles on the lee-side of the saloon bunks and trying to sleep amid the chill seething, roaring, and thudding. The miner, young, powerful, and very much at his ease, sprawled among them intoxicated. He sang, and continued to sing at intervals, a song about 'The hat that my father wore,' swaying, with large dreamy gestures, to and fro, round and about, up and down upon the unfortunate men sitting to right and left of him. Close at hand sat another young man, but smaller, who carried a big brass trumpet.

'Throw him in the sea, why not, now!' the

trumpeter shouted to the drunken man's weary supporters. 'Begad, I would do it if he put his pig's face on e'er a shoulder of me!' He was a small, emphatic young man: 'Give him a crack now, and lay on him, or by the tears of God we'll get no repose at all!'

His advice was tendered as constantly and as insistently as the miner's song about his parent's headgear, and he would encourage these incitements to vicarious violence by putting the brass trumpet to his lips and blowing some bitter and not very accurate staves. So bitter and so inaccurate that at length even the drunken miner paused in his song and directed the trumpeter to 'shut up'. The little man sprang to his feet in fury, and approaching the other he poured a succession of trumpet calls close into his face. This threw the miner into a deep sleep, a result so unexpected that the enraged trumpeter slung his instrument under his arm and pranced belligerently upon the deck.

'Come out o' that, ye drunken matchbox, and by the Queen of Heaven I'll teach ye! Come now!'

The miner momentarily raised himself and recommenced his song: ''Tis the hat that me father wore!' At this the trumpeter fetched him a mighty slap across the face.

F—AE   [137]

'Ah, go away,' groaned the miner, 'or I'll be sick on ye.'

'Try it, ye rotten gossoon! ye filthy matchbox! Where's yer khar*kee*?'

The miner could display no khaki; indeed, he was sleeping deeply again.

'I'm a man o' me principles, ye rotten matchbox!' yelled the trumpeter. 'In the Munsters I was . . . seven years . . . where's your khar*kee*?'

He seized the miner by the collar and shook that part of the steamer into a new commotion until he was collared by the sailors and kicked up on to the foredeck.

Nothing up there, not even his futile trumpeting, could disturb the chill rejoicing beauty of the night. The wind increased, but the moonlight was bland and reassuring. Often the cope of some tall wave would plunge dully over the bows, filling the deck with water that floundered foaming with the ship's movement or dribbled back through the scuppers into the sea. Yet there was no menace in the dark wandering water; each wave tossed back from its neck a wreath of foam that slewed like milk across the breast of its follower.

The trumpeter sat upon a heap of ropes beside a big soldier.

'The rotten matchbox, did ye ever see the like o' that?' I'll kill him against the first thing we step ashore, like ye would a flea!'

'Be aisy!' said the soldier. 'Why are ye making trouble at all? Have ye hurt your little finger?'

'Trouble, is it? What way would I be making trouble in this world?' exclaimed the trumpeter. 'Isn't it the world itself as puts trouble on ye, so it is, like a wild cat sitting under a tub of unction! O, very pleasant it is, O ay! No, no, my little sojee, that is not it at all. You can't let the flaming world rush beyant ye like that. . . .'

'Well, it's a quiet life I'm seeking,' interjected the soldier, wrapping his greatcoat comfortingly across his breast, 'and by this and by that, a quiet night too.'

'Is that so? Quiet, is it? But I say, my little sojee, you'll not get it at all and the whole flaming world whickering at ye like a mad cracker itself. Would ye sleep on that wid yer quiet life and all? It's to tame life you'd be doing, like it was a tiger. And it's no drunken bouzer can tame me as was with the Munsters in the East . . . for seven holy years.'

'Ah, go off wid you; you've hurt your little finger.'

'Me little finger, is it?' cried the trumpeter, holding his thin hands up for inspection in the moonlight. 'I have not, then.'

'You surprise me,' the soldier said, gazing at him with sleepy amused tolerance. 'Did you ever hear of Tobin the smith and Mary of Cappoquin?'

'I did not, then,' snapped the other. 'Who was they?'

'He was a roaring, fatal feller, a holy terror, a giant. He lived in the mountains, but he went over the country killing things—a tiger or two at an odd time, I'm thinking—and destroying the neat condition of the world. And he had a nasty little bit of a bugle. . . .'

'Was it the like o' that?' demanded the other, holding out the trumpet and tapping it with his fingers.

' "A bugle," I said,' replied the soldier sternly, 'and every time he puffed in its tubes the noise of it was so severe the hens in the town fell dead. . . .'

'The hens?'

'Yes, and the ducks on the ponds were overcome with emotion and sank to the bottom. One day he was in his forge driving a few nails into the shoe of an ass when he hit his little finger such a blow, a terrible blow, that it bled for a day. Then he seared the wound with his searing iron, but it was no better, and it bled for a night. I will go—says he —to the physician of Cappoquin and be sewn up with some golden wire. So he drove into Cappoquin, but when he was in it the physician was gone to a christening; there was only his daughter Mary left to attend to him, a bright good girl entirely, and when she saw the finger she said to Tobin: "I declare on my soul if I don't chop it off it's not long till you have your death." "Chop it off, then," says Tobin, and she did so. He came back the next day and this is how it was; the physician was gone to a wake. "What's your need?" asked Mary. He showed her his hand and it dripping with blood. "I declare to my God," said Mary, "if I don't chop if off it's short till you have your death." "Chop it off," says Tobin, and she struck off the hand. The day after that he drove in again, but the physician was gone to an inquest about a little matter concerning some remains that had been found. "What is it to-day, Tobin?" and he showed her his arm bleeding in great drops. "I declare by the saints," says she, "that unless I chop it off you'll die in five minutes." "Chop it off," says Tobin, and she struck off his arm. The next day he was back again with the stump of his arm worse than before. 'Oh, I see what it is,'' said Mary, and going behind him she struck off his head with one blow of her father's sharp knife and gave it to the cat.'

'That is a neat tale,' said the trumpeter. 'Did you hear the story of the dirty soldier and the drummer?'

'No—' The soldier hesitated reflectively. 'No, I never heard it.'

'Well, this is how it was. . . .'

But just then the steamer began to approach the harbour, and in the hurry and scurry of preparations to land the two friends were separated and the tale was never told.

At the disembarkation passengers and soldiers crowded on the pier awaiting the boat train. The harbour was full of lights; the moon was still high in the heavens, but her glory faded as the sun began to rise. The thick densities of the night sky quivered into frail blues, violet and silver were mingled in the sea, the buildings on the wharf looked strange; icily, bitterly grey. The trumpeter ran about in the bleak air seeking the 'rotten match-box', but he could not find him. He comforted himself by executing some castigating blares upon his instrument. The hollow wharves and the pier staging echoed with acrid sound that pleased his

[142]

simple heart. He blew and blew and blew until he was surrounded by people watching him strain his determined eyes and inflate his pale cheeks—all of them secretly hoping that the ones might fall out or the others might crack. Suddenly he caught sight of the now-sobered miner, quite close to him, almost touching him! The call he was blowing faded with a stupid squeak. The world began to flame again . . . when an officer burst into the circle, demanding to know who he was, where from, and what in all the realm of blasphemous things he meant by tootling in that infernal manner on that infernal thing.

The trumpeter drew himself proudly to attention and saluted.

'Discharged I am, sir; it's with the Munsters I was, seven years, sir, with the Munsters, in the east.'

'You disgrace to the Army! If I hear another tootle on that thing, I . . . I'll have you clapped in irons—I will! And . . . and transported . . . damn me if I don't! You understand?'

The trumpeter meekly saluted as the captain swaggered away. At that moment the miner laid his hand upon his arm.

'What, my little man,' said he, 'have you lost your teeth? Give it me now!'

And putting the trumpet to his own lips he blew a brilliant and mocking reveille, whose echoes hurtled far over the harbour and into the neighbouring hills.

'God save us!' cried the trumpeter with a furtive eye on the captain at the end of the platform, who did not appear to have heard that miraculous salvo, 'it's a great grand breath you've got, sir.'

THE ANGEL AND THE SWEEP

I'D been sitting in the *Axe and Cleaver* along of Mrs. Pellegrini for an hour at least; I hadn't seen her in five years since she was doing the roads near Pontypool. An hour at least, for isn't the *Axe and Cleaver* the pleasant kind of place? Talking or not talking you can always hear the water lashing from the outfall above Hinney Lock, the sound of it making you feel drowsy and kind. And isn't the old bridge there a thing to be looking at indeed?

Mrs. Pellegrini had a family of pikeys who traded in horses, willow-wattles, and rocksalt; she was as cunning as a jacksnipe, and if she *had* a deep voice like a man she was full of wisdom. A grand great woman was Rosa Pellegrini, with a face silky-brown like a beechnut, and eyes and hair the equal of a rook for darkness. The abundance of jewellery hooked and threaded upon her was something to be looking at too. Old man and young Isaac kept going out to look at the horses, or they'd be coming in to upbraid her for delaying, but she could drink a sconce of beer without the least sparkle of hilarity, as if it were a tribute she owed her whole magnificent constitution, or at least a reward for some part of it. So she kept doing it, while her son and her husband could do no other and did it with nothing of her inevitable air.

Well, I was sitting in the *Axe and Cleaver* along of Mrs. Pellegrini when who should rove in but Larry McCall, good-looking Larry, bringing a friend with him, a soft kind of fellow who'd a harsh voice and a whining voice that we didn't like the noise of tho' he had good money in his purse. Larry gave me the grace of the day directly he entered the door, and then, letting a cry of joy out of him, he'd kissed Mrs. Pellegrini many times before she knew what was happening to her. She got up and punished him with a welt on his chin that would have bruised an oak-tree, and bade him behave himself. He sat down soothingly beside her and behaved very well. His companion stood very shy and nervous, like a kitten might be watching a cock-fight.

'Who is this young man?' Mrs. Pellegrini asks.

'That's Arthur,' said Larry: 'I forget what Arthur knocks a living out of—I've known him but these three bits of an hour since we were walking in the one direction.'

'My dad,' said Arthur slowly and raspingly, 'is an

undertaker, and he lets me help him in his business:
we bury people.'

'Oh, come, young man,' said Mrs. Pellegrini,
'that's no sort of a trade at all—d'ye think it, Mr.
McCall?'

'No, I do not,' replied Larry, 'but Arthur does.
It don't seem to be a trade with very much humour
in it. Life ain't a sad solid chunk.'

'Now that's just where you're wrong,' drawled
Arthur.

''Tain't a life at all,' Rosa interrupted severely,
'it's only sniffing, having a bad cold! No sort of a
life at all—d'ye think it, Mr. McCall?'

'No, I do not,' said Larry with a chuckle, 'but
Arthur does!'

'Oh, I know what you're a deluding on,' commenced the young man again, 'but . . .'

'Strike me dead if I can see any fun in funerals!'
Mrs. Pellegrini said with finality, taking up her
mug. 'But if you *will* have your grief, young man,'
she added, pausing in one of her gulps to gaze at
Arthur until he quivered, 'you must have it, and
may fortune fall in love with what we like. Fill up
that cup now!'

The young man in agitation obeyed, and while
this was doing we all heard some one come over the

bridge singing a song, and that was Jerry Ogwin, who could tell the neatest tales and sing the littlest songs. Well, there were great salutations, for we all knew Jerry and loved Jerry, and he loved some of us. But he was the fiercest-looking, fieriest gipsy man you ever saw, and he had all the gullible prescience of a Cockney.

'My fortune! Where are you from, you cunning little man?'

'I bin doing a bit o' road down Kent and London way. D'ye know Lewisham?' commenced Jerry.

'No,' said Larry, grinning at me, 'but Arthur does!'

'No, I don't; I never been there,' chanted Arthur.

'Now what's the good of talking like that!' said McCall sternly, and letting a wink at me.

'More I ain't,' asserted Arthur.

'Then I was at Deptford and Greenwich—know Greenwich?' continued Jerry.

'No,' replied Larry, then adding nonchalantly, 'Arthur does.'

'No, I don't, I don't,' said Arthur wormily, for Jerry was glaring at him, and that fighting scar all down his nose, where his wife Katey once hit him with the spout of a kettle, was very disturbing.

'What's the good of that?' urged the devilish-minded Larry. 'Why don't you talk to the gentleman? You don't want to vex him, do you?'

'You ain't blooming silly, are you?' queried Jerry.

Without waiting for reply he drifted off again.

'Me and my mate was doing a bit o' road with oranges and things, you know—three for a 'eaver—down Mary's Cray; d'ye know Mary's Cray?'

But this time Arthur was looking avidly out of the window.

'Well, we was 'avin' a bit of grub one night, just about dark it was, *you* know, with a little fire, we'd bin cookin' something, when a blooming sweep come along. I'll tell it to you; it was just inside a bit of a wood and we was sleeping rough. My mate was a bit nervous, *you* know, 'e kept looking round as if 'e could see something, but it was that dark you might be looking in a sack. I says to Timmy: What's up with you? I dunno, 'e says, something going on, and just as 'e says that this blooming sweep 'oofs in from nowhere and falls over our beer. I says to Timmy: 'E's knocked over our beer; are you going to fight 'im or shall I? And Timmy shouts: Look at 'im, 'e's laying on the fire! And s'elp me God so 'e was, 'is legs was in

the sticks and 'is trousers was a-burning. Come out
of it, we says, but 'e didn't move. No, my oath, 'e
layed there like a dead sheep. Well, we pulled 'im
off it, but 'e was like a silly bloke. 'E couldn't
stand up and 'e couldn't say anything. 'E got a lot
of froth round 'is mouth like a 'orse that's going
wicked. And 'e wasn't drunk, neither, but, *you*
know, 'e was just frightened out of 'is life about
something. We sit 'im down with 'is back against
a tree and made the fire up again. What's the matter
with you, we says; you got a fit, we says; what d'ye
want coming 'ere, we says? But we couldn't get
no answer from 'im. 'Is face was that dam white
'cept where it was smudged with soot, and there
was this froth dribbling on 'im, and what d'yer
think, 'e'd got a red rose stuck in 'is button-'ole.
'E was a horrible sight; we couldn't bear 'im, so
we picks 'im up, and Timmy give 'im a clout in the
ear and shoves 'im out among some bushes where we
couldn't see 'im. Sw'elp me if 'e didn't come
crawling back on 'is hands and knees where we
was sitting round the fire. Oh, 'e was horrible.
Timmy went nearly daft and I thought 'e was going
to give 'im one good kick in the mouth and finish
'im. 'Stead of that we picks 'im up again and runs
'im further down the wood and heaves 'im into

some blackberry bushes and tells 'im what we'd do to 'im if 'e come again. That was no good; in five minutes 'e crawled back. Timmy was shaking like a dog, and fell on 'im as if 'e was going to strangle 'im, but we had to let 'im stay, and old Timmy was blacker than the sweep when 'e'd done with 'im. But the bloke wouldn't say nothing or open 'is eyes, *you* know, he *wouldn't* open his eyes, 'e was like something what had been murdered and wouldn't die, if you know what I mean. Blast 'im, I could kill 'im, Timmy says. That's no good of, says I, and at last we left 'im 'side the fire, and we went off somewhere just outside the wood and packed up in a clump of ur-grass. I went to sleep, but I don't believe old Timmy did; well, I know 'e didn't. Now we hadn't 'eard nothing all night, nothing at all, but when I wakes up in the morning the blooming sweep was gone and not a chink of 'im left anywhere. But,' said Jerry impressively to Arthur, who eyed him with horror, 'we found something else!' There was silence while Jerry's face was connected to his mug of beer. Nobody spoke. We eyed him with eager interest. He vanquished his thirst and smacked his lips, but held the mug in readiness for further libation.

'Not twenty chain away a woman was laying

down. Timmy touches me frightened like and says, Look, what's that? My eyes was nearly skinned out of me. I couldn't speak. We walked quietly up to 'er like two sick men. She lay there just as if she'd dropped out of the sky, naked as an angel, not a shift nor a stocking, not a button on 'er.' There was again silence until Larry struck a match loudly on a jar, his pipe, hooked tightly in his fore-finger, having gone out. Mrs. Pellegrini stared, and breathed audibly. 'And,' said Jerry impressively, 'she was the grandest creature what ever you see. I touched 'er with them two fingers and she was cold as iron, stiff, gone a bit dull like pearls look, but the fine build of that lady was the world's wonder. There was not a scratch or a wound on 'er or the sign of 'er death anywhere. One of 'er legs was cocked up at the knee like she'd lay in bed. 'Er two eyes was just looking at the ground and there was a kind of funny smile on 'er face. Fine long hair she had, black as a cat's back and long as the tail of a horse. And in it there was a red rose, and in one of 'er hands she was holding a white lily. There was a little bird's dropping on 'er stomach. I wiped it off. I says to Timmy: That sweep! And 'e says to me, Jerry Ogwin, we're 'aving a share out. What about that sweep, I says to 'im, but all 'e says was:

We're 'aving a share out. 'E was afraid of getting pulled for this job, *you* know. I never seen a man so frightened afore, and 'e was not a chap as re-nagged ever, not Timmy.'

'That 'e wasn't,' said Mrs. Pellegrini. 'I seen 'im once half murder two sojers for beating a deaf and dumb man.'

'Well,' continued Jerry, 'I says all right, Timmy, and so we 'as a share out and gits on different roads. My share was a clothes basket and a pair of spectacles cost tuppence ha'penny, *you* know, and I walked all that day as 'ard as ever I could. Then I bushes for the night, and when I woke up nex' morning I 'eard some talking going on. I looks under the 'edge and found I was side a strawberry field, *you* know, a lot of strawberries. So I 'ops in and sells my basket to the strawberry pickers for a shilling. They give me a shilling for it, so that was all right. 'Ad a shilling and a pair of spectacles for my share out. I goes on a bit and then I comes across a bean-feast party, and I showed 'em my pair o' gold spectacles—I'd just found 'em—*you* know!'

Larry burst into a peal of laughter that seemed to surprise Jerry and he said:

'Ain't you ever met a feller what's found a pair of gold spectacles?'

Larry couldn't reply and Jerry continued:

'No, ain't you really? God, what a laugh! Yes, I sells 'em to a fly young party for two and fo'pence and off I goes. Never 'eard no more of Timmy. Never 'eard no more of anything. I dunno if they found the girl. I dunno if they found that sweep. They didn't find *me*.'

He paused for a moment.

'They didn't find *me*,' he repeated.

There was silence at last; the room was getting dim with evening. Mrs. Pellegrini spoke:

'And you wiped it off her stomach, did you, Jerry?'

'I did,' said he.

Mrs. Pellegrini turned to Arthur and said in a sharp voice:

'Fill that pot for the gentleman!'

The young man in terror obeyed, he exceedingly obeyed.

When the last pot was emptied Jerry and Larry and the wretched mute went off along the road together. Rosa Pellegrini said 'So long' to me and drove off with her cavalcade. The inn was empty and quiet again so you could hear the water at the outfall.

I walked along the bank of the old river until

I came to the lock where the water roaring windily from the lasher streamed like an old man's beard; a pair of swans moved in the slack water of the pool. Away there was a fine lea of timothy grass looking as soft as wool. And at the end of the lea there was a low long hill covered with trees full of the arriving darkness; a train that you could not hear the noise of shot through a grove and poured a long spool of white fume upon the trees quietly, a thing to be looking at, it was so white and soft. But I was thinking . . . thinking . . . thinking of the grand white slim woman who did not seem dead at all to me, lying with a lily in her hand, a red rose in her hair. And I could not think it to be true at all; I believe Jerry was only telling us one of his tales.

ARABESQUE: *THE MOUSE*

In the main street amongst tall establishments of mart and worship was a high narrow house pressed between a coffee factory and a bootmaker's. It had four flights of long dim echoing stairs, and at the top, in a room that was full of the smell of dried apples and mice, a man in the middle age of life had sat reading Russian novels until he thought he was mad. Late was the hour, the night outside black and freezing, the pavements below empty and undistinguishable when he closed his book and sat motionless in front of the glowing but flameless fire. He felt he was very tired, yet he could not rest. He stared at a picture on the wall until he wanted to cry; it was a colour-print by Utamaro of a suckling child caressing its mother's breasts as she sits in front of a blackbound mirror. Very chaste and decorative it was, in spite of its curious anatomy. The man gazed, empty of sight though not of mind, until the sighing of the gas-jet maddened him. He got up, put out the light, and sat down again in the darkness trying to compose his mind before the comfort of the fire. And he was just about to begin a conversation with himself when a mouse crept from a hole in the skirting near the fireplace and scurried into the fender. The man had the crude dislike for such sly nocturnal things, but this mouse was so small and bright, its antics so pretty, that he drew his feet carefully from the fender and sat watching it almost with amusement. The mouse moved along the shadows of the fender, out upon the hearth, and sat before the glow, rubbing its head, ears, and tiny belly with its paws as if it were bathing itself with the warmth, until, sharp and sudden, the fire sank, an ember fell, and the mouse flashed into its hole.

The man reached forward to the mantelpiece and put his hand upon a pocket lamp. Turning on the beam, he opened the door of a cupboard beside the fireplace. Upon one of the shelves there was a small trap baited with cheese, a trap made with a wire spring, one of those that smashed down to break the back of ingenuous and unwary mice.

'Mean—so mean,' he mused, 'to appeal to the hunger of any living thing just in order to destroy it.'

He picked up the empty trap as if to throw it in the fire.

'I suppose I had better leave it though—the place

swarms with them.' He still hesitated. 'I hope that little beastie won't go and do anything foolish.' He put the trap back quite carefully, closed the door of the cupboard, sat down again and extinguished the lamp.

Was there anyone else in the world so squeamish and foolish about such things! Even his mother, mother so bright and beautiful, even she had laughed at his childish horrors. He recalled how once in his childhood, not long after his sister Yosine was born, a friendly neighbour had sent him home with a bundle of dead larks tied by the feet 'for supper'. The pitiful inanimity of the birds had brought a gush of tears; he had run weeping home and into the kitchen, and there he had found the strange thing doing. It was dusk; mother was kneeling before the fire. He dropped the larks.

'Mother!' he exclaimed softly.

She looked at his tearful face.

'What's the matter, Filip?' she asked, smiling too at his astonishment.

'Mother! What you doing?'

Her bodice was open and she was squeezing her breasts; long thin streams of milk spurted into the fire with a plunging noise.

'Weaning your little sister,' laughed mother.

She took his inquisitive face and pressed it against the delicate warmth of her bosom, and he forgot the dead birds behind him.

'Let me do it, mother,' he cried, and doing so he discovered the throb of the heart in his mother's breast. Wonderful it was for him to experience it, although she could not explain it to him.

'Why does it do that?'

'If it did not beat, little son, I should die and the Holy Father would take me from you.'

'God?'

She nodded. He put his hand upon his own breast. 'Oh, feel it, Mother!' he cried. Mother unbuttoned his little coat and felt the gentle *tick tick* with her warm palm.

'Beautiful!' she said.

'Is it a good one?'

She kissed his smiling lips. 'It is good if it beats truly. Let it always beat truly, Filip; let it always beat truly.'

There was the echo of a sigh in her voice, and he had divined some grief, for he was very wise. He kissed her bosom in his tiny ecstasy and whispered soothingly: 'Little mother! little mother!' In such joys he forgot his horror of the dead larks; indeed he helped mother to pluck them and spit them for supper.

It was a black day that succeeded, and full of tragedy for the child. A great bay horse with a tawny mane had knocked down his mother in the lane, and a heavy cart had passed over her, crushing both her hands. She was borne away moaning with anguish to the surgeon who cut off the two hands. She died in the night. For years the child's dreams were filled with the horror of the stumps of arms, bleeding unendingly. Yet he had never seen them, for he was sleeping when she died.

While this old woe was come vividly before him he again became aware of the mouse. His nerves stretched upon him in repulsion, but he soon relaxed to a tolerant interest, for it was really a most engaging little mouse. It moved with curious staccato scurries, stopping to rub its head or flicker with its ears; they seemed almost transparent ears. It spied a red cinder and skipped innocently up to it . . . sniffing . . . sniffing . . . until it jumped back scorched. It would crouch as a cat does, blinking in the warmth, or scamper madly as if dancing, and then roll upon its side rubbing its head with those pliant paws. The melancholy man watched it until it came at last to rest and squatted meditatively upon its haunches, hunched up, looking curiously wise, a pennyworth of philosophy; then once more the coals sank with a rattle and again the mouse was gone.

The man sat on before the fire and his mind filled again with unaccountable sadness. He had grown into manhood with a burning generosity of spirit and rifts of rebellion in him that proved too exacting for his fellows and seemed mere wantonness to men of casual rectitudes. 'Justice and Sin,' he would cry, 'Property and Virtue—incompatibilities! There can be no sin in a world of justice, no property in a world of virtue!' With an engaging extravagance and a certain clear-eyed honesty of mind he had put his two and two together and seemed then to rejoice, as in some topsy-turvy dream, in having rendered unto Cæsar, as you might say, the things that were due to Napoleon! But this kind of thing could not pass unexpiated in a world of men having an infinite regard for Property and a pride in their traditions of Virtue and Justice. They could indeed forgive him his sins, but they could not forgive him his compassions. So he had to go seek for more melodious-minded men and fair unambiguous women. But rebuffs can deal more deadly blows than daggers; he became timid—a timidity not of fear but of pride—and grew with the years into misanthropy, susceptible to trivial griefs and despairs, a vessel of emotion that emptied as easily as it filled, until he came at last to know that his griefs were half deliberate, his despairs half unreal, and to live but for beauty—which is tranquillity—to put her wooing hand upon him.

Now, while the mouse hunts in the cupboard, one fair recollection stirs in the man's mind—of Cassia and the harmony of their only meeting, Cassia who had such rich red hair, and eyes, yes, her eyes were full of starry inquiry like the eyes of mice. It was so long ago that he had forgotten how he came to be in it, that unaccustomed orbit of vain vivid things—a village festival, all oranges and houpla. He could not remember how he came to be there, but at night, in the court hall, he had danced with Cassia—fair and unambiguous indeed!—who had come like the wind from among the roses and swept into his heart.

'It is easy to guess,' he had said to her, 'what you like most in the world.'

She laughed. 'To dance? Yes, and you . . .?'

'To find a friend.'

'I know, I know,' she cried, caressing him with recognitions. 'Ah, at times I quite love my friends —until I begin to wonder how much they hate me!'

He had loved at once that cool pale face, the

abundance of her strange hair as light as the autumn's clustered bronze, her lilac dress and all the sweetness about her like a bush of lilies. How they had laughed at the two old peasants whom they had overheard gabbling of trifles like sickness and appetite!

'There's a lot of nature in a parsnip,' said one, a fat person of the kind that swells grossly when stung by a bee, 'a lot of nature when it's young, but when it's old it's like everything else.'

'True it is.'

'And I'm very fond of vegetables, yes, and I'm very fond of bread.'

'Come out with me,' whispered Cassia to Filip, and they walked out in the blackness of midnight into what must have been a garden.

'Cool it is here,' she said, 'and quiet, but too dark even to see your face—can you see mine?'

'The moon will not rise until after dawn,' said he, 'it will be white in the sky when the starlings whistle in your chimney.'

They walked silently and warily about until they felt the chill of the air. A dull echo of the music came to them through the walls, then stopped, and they heard the bark of a fox away in the woods.

'You are cold,' he whispered, touching her bare

[163]

neck with timid fingers. 'Quite, quite cold,' drawing his hand tenderly over the curves of her chin and face. 'Let us go in,' he said, moving with discretion from the rapture he desired. 'We will come out again,' said Cassia.

But within the room the ball was just at an end, the musicians were packing up their instruments and the dancers were flocking out and homewards, or to the buffet which was on a platform at one end of the room. The two old peasants were there, munching hugely.

'I tell you,' said one of them, 'there's nothing in the world for it but the grease of an owl's liver. That's it, that's it! Take something on your stomach now, just to offset the chill of the dawn!'

Filip and Cassia were beside them, but there were so many people crowding the platform that Filip had to jump down. He stood then looking up adoringly at Cassia, who had pulled a purple cloak around her.

'For Filip, Filip, Filip,' she said, pushing the last bite of her sandwich into his mouth, and pressing upon him her glass of Loupiac. Quickly he drank it with a great gesture, and, flinging the glass to the wall, took Cassia into his arms, shouting: 'I'll carry you home, the whole way home, yes, I'll carry you!'

'Put me down!' she cried, beating his head and pulling his ears, as they passed among the departing dancers. 'Put me down, you wild thing!'

Dark, dark was the lane outside, and the night an obsidian net, into which he walked carrying the girl. But her arms were looped around him; she discovered paths for him, clinging more tightly as he staggered against a wall, stumbled upon a gulley, or when her sweet hair was caught in the boughs of a little lime tree.

'Do not loose me, Filip, will you? Do not loose me,' Cassia said, putting her lips against his temple.

His brain seemed bursting, his heart rocked within him, but he adored the rich grace of her limbs against his breast. 'Here it is,' she murmured, and he carried her into a path that led to her home in a little lawned garden where the smell of ripe apples upon the branches and the heavy lustre of roses stole upon the air. Roses and apples! Roses and apples! He carried her right into the porch before she slid down and stood close to him with her hands still upon his shoulders. He could breathe happily at the release, standing silent and looking round at the sky sprayed with wondrous stars but without a moon.

'You are stronger than I thought you, stronger

than you look; you are really very strong,' she whispered, nodding her head to him. Opening the buttons of his coat, she put her palm against his breast.

'Oh, how your heart does beat! Does it beat truly—and for whom?'

He had seized her wrists in a little fury of love, crying: 'Little mother, little mother!'

'What are you saying?' asked the girl; but before he could continue there came a footstep sounding behind the door, and the clack of a bolt. . . .

What was that? Was that really a bolt or was it . . . was it . . . the snap of the trap? The man sat up in his room intently listening, with nerves quivering again, waiting for the trap to kill the little philosopher. When he felt it was all over he reached guardedly in the darkness for the lantern, turned on the beam, and opened the door of the cupboard. Focussing the light upon the trap, he was amazed to see the mouse sitting on its haunches before it, uncaught. It head was bowed, but its bead-like eyes were full of brightness, and it sat blinking, it did not flee.

'Shoosh!' said the man, but the mouse did not move. 'Why doesn't it go? Shoosh!' he said again, and suddenly the reason of the mouse's strange behaviour was made clear. The trap had not caught it completely, but it had broken off both its fore-feet, and the thing crouched there holding out its two bleeding stumps humanly, too stricken to stir.

Horror flooded the man, and conquering his repugnance he plucked the mouse up quickly by the neck. Immediately the little thing fastened its teeth in his finger; the touch was no more than the slight prick of a pin. The man's impulse then ex-hausted itself. What should he do with it? He put his hand behind him, he dared not look, but there was nothing to be done except kill it at once, quickly, quickly. Oh, how should he do it? He bent towards the fire as if to drop the mouse into its quenching glow; but he paused and shuddered, he would hear its cries, he would have to listen. Should he crush it with finger and thumb? A glance towards the window decided him. He opened the sash with one hand and flung the wounded mouse far into the dark street. Closing the window with a crash, he sank into a chair, limp with pity too deep for tears.

So he sat for two minutes, five minutes, ten minutes. Anxiety and shame filled him with heat. He opened the window again, and the freezing air poured in and cooled him. Seizing his lantern, he ran down the echoing stairs, into the dark empty street, searching long and vainly for the little philosopher until he had to desist and return to his room, shivering, frozen to his very bones.

When he had recovered some warmth he took the trap from its shelf. The two feet dropped into his hand; he cast them into the fire. Then he once more set the trap and put it back carefully into the cupboard.